"That's not p...
Isabelle mur...

Their eyes met, and Connor's were full of questions. "My family isn't in my life at the moment," she admitted. The enormity of the situation came crashing over her. Despite being at an event crowded with people, Isabelle was achingly alone.

"Oh, Ella. Please don't cry. It's going to be all right." Connor quickly swallowed up the distance between them and put his arms around her. She let out a muffled sob against his chest. She felt his hand moving on her back as he murmured soothing words. It was comforting to be held by him.

Isabelle breathed in his woodsy, masculine scent. Although she knew it wasn't possible, she didn't want this moment to end. It had been a long time since someone had made her feel safe and protected. For so long now she had been trying to protect her family members from harm as well as herself. It was nice to take shelter, if only for a little while, in Connor's arms…

Belle Calhoune grew up in a small town in Massachusetts. Married to her college sweetheart, she is raising two lovely daughters in Connecticut. A dog lover, she has one mini poodle and a black Lab. Writing for the Love Inspired line is a dream come true. Working at home in her pajamas is one of the best perks of the job. Belle enjoys summers in Cape Cod, traveling and reading.

Books by Belle Calhoune

Love Inspired

Home to Owl Creek

Her Secret Alaskan Family
Alaskan Christmas Redemption
An Alaskan Twin Surprise
Hiding in Alaska

Alaskan Grooms

An Alaskan Wedding
Alaskan Reunion
A Match Made in Alaska
Reunited at Christmas
His Secret Alaskan Heiress
An Alaskan Christmas
Her Alaskan Cowboy

Reunited with the Sheriff
Forever Her Hero
Heart of a Soldier

Visit the Author Profile page at Harlequin.com.

Hiding in Alaska

Belle Calhoune

LOVE INSPIRED

INSPIRATIONAL ROMANCE

If you purchased this book without a cover you should be aware that this book is stolen property. It was reported as "unsold and destroyed" to the publisher, and neither the author nor the publisher has received any payment for this "stripped book."

LOVE INSPIRED®
INSPIRATIONAL ROMANCE

Recycling programs for this product may not exist in your area.

ISBN-13: 978-1-335-43086-1

Hiding in Alaska

Copyright © 2021 by Sandra Calhoune

All rights reserved. No part of this book may be used or reproduced in any manner whatsoever without written permission except in the case of brief quotations embodied in critical articles and reviews.

This is a work of fiction. Names, characters, places and incidents are either the product of the author's imagination or are used fictitiously. Any resemblance to actual persons, living or dead, businesses, companies, events or locales is entirely coincidental.

This edition published by arrangement with Harlequin Books S.A.

For questions and comments about the quality of this book, please contact us at CustomerService@Harlequin.com.

Love Inspired
22 Adelaide St. West, 40th Floor
Toronto, Ontario M5H 4E3, Canada
www.Harlequin.com

Printed in U.S.A.

He healeth the broken in heart,
and bindeth up their wounds.
He telleth the number of the stars;
he calleth them all by their names.
—*Psalms* 147:3–4

To my beloved neighbor, Rosalie "Rose" Healey
(1926–2019).
One of the kindest, loveliest people
I've ever known. A wonderful friend. Missing you.

Chapter One

Isabelle Sanchez shivered as the cold Arctic wind whipped against her cheeks. This type of weather would certainly take some getting used to, she thought as she wrapped her arms around her middle. She didn't feel at all like herself in the navy blue parka with the fur-trimmed hood. A wool hat was perched on her head, covering her ears from the frigid temperatures. It was the first time in her life she'd ever owned a thick winter coat and it felt cumbersome and unnatural. She was far more used to wearing shorts, shades and sundresses.

Bathing suits rather than boots. There was no point in dwelling on it. She had agreed to come live in this Alaskan hamlet, and there was no going back.

A sigh slipped past her lips. Her entire life had changed in an instant, and it still felt surreal. The sign by the side of the road said it best: *Welcome to Owl Creek, Alaska.* The harsh reality of her situation caused her to suck in a steadying breath. She would need to call on every ounce of strength she had in order to rebuild her life. There was no doubt in her mind it would be the hardest thing she'd ever do.

She wasn't Isabelle Sanchez from Miami, Florida, anymore. Now, as part of the Witness Protection Program, she was Ella Perez from Flagstaff, Arizona. She felt a sudden chill pass over her that had nothing to do with the frigid weather. WITSEC—the United States Federal Witness Protection Program—had provided her with a new identity and placed her in Owl Creek, a remote Alaskan town she'd never heard of until a few weeks ago. It appeared to be a charming and picturesque village, unlike anything she'd ever known. She was a Floridian, born and bred. Sandy beaches, sunny skies, and the hustle and bustle of city life were the norm for her. The sight of white-capped mountains looming in the distance served as a breathtaking reminder that she wasn't in the Sunshine State any longer. She no longer had a home, and it made her heartsick just thinking about it.

Her life had been forever altered by the events of a few months ago. Even though she was trying to be strong, Isabelle was afraid. She'd never wanted to be so far away from her loved ones. She had left everything she held dear back in Miami—family, friends and a job she enjoyed. It was the first time in her life she'd ever felt all alone. She didn't know the slightest thing about life in a small Alaskan town. But she didn't have a choice in the matter. Isabelle had to make it work here in Owl Creek. Her very life hung in the balance.

"The truck is over there in the lot. It's time we headed over to your new home." The deep voice interrupted her thoughts, and she swung her gaze in the direction of the tall, ginger-haired man who had accompanied her all the way from Miami. Despite his gruff demeanor, U.S. Marshal Jonah Kramer had a streak of kindness that meant the world to Isabelle. It's what she needed most at this moment as she faced an uncertain future. Over the past few weeks he'd tried to reassure Isabelle at every step in the process. She felt a tad guilty about taking him away from his wife and family in Homer, but she knew it was simply part of his job to help her relocate.

Once they were sitting in the hunter

green truck with Jonah in the driver's seat, he turned toward her. "You'll be safe here, Ella. Just try to blend in with the townsfolk. I know it's hard to wrap your head around it, but you can't contact anyone from your former life under any circumstances. We've drilled that into your head, but it bears repeating. It's crucial to make a clean break from everything and everyone. If you slip up, it could be catastrophic."

Isabelle nodded. She knew the drill. It was the most heartbreaking aspect of her joining WITSEC. Just the thought of never seeing her family again caused tears to well up in her eyes.

Ella. She would have to get adjusted to her new name. Although she'd been allowed to assume a first name that wasn't too far off from her own, it would still take some getting used to, since no one had ever called her Ella. Her nickname had always been Izzy. Her head was spinning with all the things she had to get acclimated to in her new surroundings.

The situation she found herself in was far from ideal, but after witnessing the brutal slaying of her boss, Saul Martino, in a turf war, her world had spiraled out of control. By God's grace she had been spared. Because the killer, Vincent Burke, had locked eyes with her before she fled the club, he had known her identity when she'd reported him to the police. Threats and attempts to silence her had ensued, turning her mundane life into a chaos-filled existence. And even after she'd provided testimony in his trial that had put him in prison, she had still been in jeopardy from his criminal enterprise. There had been numerous attempts on her life that left her feeling terrorized and vulnerable. She would never again be safe in her former life. Those extreme circumstances had led her straight to the quaint town of Owl Creek.

The wintry Alaskan scenery passed by in a blur as Jonah drove them to her new residence. When they pulled up to 10 Kodiak Lane, a sigh escaped Isabelle's lips. She was instantly charmed by the log cabin–style house. It radiated a cozy vibe. Snow-covered bushes surrounded a wraparound porch. Two sturdy Adirondack chairs sat on the front porch. Although she had never fantasized about living in Alaska, this picture-perfect house was the stuff of dreams.

Once the car was in Park, Isabelle got out of the vehicle and walked up to the porch, bags in hand. Isabelle knew she would have to make a few trips back and forth to collect all of her things from the truck, but she felt an urgent need to go inside and get settled. Jonah walked behind her, juggling a few bags before placing them on the landing and handing her a key to the house. Her hands were shaking as she reached for it. Jonah gave her an encouraging nod. When she turned the key in the lock and pushed the door open, the smell of freshly baked cookies rose to her nostrils. She stepped inside and looked around, feeling grateful for the warm atmosphere and all the beautiful little touches. A vase of baby's breath mixed with dried berries sat on the kitchen counter. A plate of chocolate chip cookies had been placed on the table with a welcome note from Beulah North, her new employer. When she pulled open the fridge, it was fully stocked with all of her favorite food and drinks. She wandered from room to room, soaking in all the details. Jonah didn't follow after her but remained in the kitchen, presumably to give her some space.

Was she really going to make a new life for herself in this small Alaskan hamlet? Isabelle still felt as if she might be dreaming as she began the process of unpacking all her bags and sorting through her belongings.

Jonah stayed until late evening to help her get settled, then he left to stay the night at a bed-and-breakfast in town called Miss Trudy's. He reminded her that he was scheduled to fly back to Homer the next morning. Fear seized her by the throat as she settled in for the night. Although she knew Jonah wouldn't be too far away in the event of an emergency, it still felt as if she was on her own.

Sometimes when she was all alone and things were quiet, Isabelle's mind flashed back to that terrible night at Club Oasis. Isabelle had worked nights at the popular dance club as its manager. When the shots rang out in the club on that particular evening, Isabelle had just locked up her office for the night. Seeing Saul's body riddled with bullets had been terrifying and surreal. Witnessing Burke standing over Saul's body with a gun in his hand had been traumatic. He was one of the most powerful men in Miami, one who'd always been tied to organized crime. Although she'd been frozen with fear, Isabelle's survival instincts had kicked in. She'd fled out the back entrance and evaded Burke's deadly aim. In the aftermath, Isabelle hadn't even had time to deal with Saul's death or her own trauma. Her entire life had imploded once she had told the police about what she'd witnessed.

"You're safe in Owl Creek now," she whispered to herself as her eyelids grew heavier and she drifted into slumber.

The next morning Isabelle drove with Jonah to the airstrip so he could catch his flight back home. On the ride over, Isabelle had the opportunity to ask him a few last-minute questions, hoping with each answer she would gain strength.

"This is where I leave you," Jonah

said as he pulled up in front of the hangar and parked the truck. "If you need anything, don't hesitate to reach out. You'll be fine."

Before she could even say an adequate goodbye, Jonah had grabbed his bag from the back seat and was walking toward the seaplane. She swallowed an instinct to call out to him and beg the U.S. Marshal to stay a little bit longer. But she knew it wasn't possible. For all intents and purposes, she was on her own. Isabelle was like a newborn baby trying to get acclimated to life outside the womb. Everything would be brand-new to her.

This entire situation was unfair. She hadn't been involved in any criminal enterprises. Isabelle had always been a law-abiding citizen. She'd simply been caught in the wrong place at the wrong time. No matter how many times she went over it in her head, it still seemed surreal. How could her life be turned upside down in an instant? Although her testimony had placed a criminal in prison, he still had the ability to get to her from the inside. And because he'd appealed his sentence, she might be forced to testify again. Would her life always be in limbo?

Isabelle scooted over and settled herself behind the driver's seat as she watched Marshal Kramer walk toward the seaplane. A heavy feeling settled on her chest. "Lord, please give me the strength to go through with this," she uttered in the stillness of the vehicle. Ever since the shooting, Isabelle had been leaning on faith to sustain her.

How would she ever get used to the quiet in this town? She was accustomed to the loud voices of her family members, the hustle and bustle of a pulsing city and the rhythms of salsa music emanating from her mother's dance studio. Owl Creek, Alaska, seemed so tame in comparison to the world she inhabited.

But wasn't that the whole point? To get away from the dangers she would be facing by continuing to live in Miami. She'd had enough drama and excitement to last her a lifetime.

It was breaking her heart to come to terms with the finality of it all. Never seeing her loved ones again would hurt worse than any pain she'd ever endured in her twenty-seven years on this earth. But she would have to suffer the agony and push through it.

"Just put one foot in front of the other," she told herself, breathing in deeply through her nose as she listened to the GPS instructions to Kodiak Lane and slowly maneuvered the truck along snow-packed roads. As she drove through the downtown area, she smiled at the sight of numerous Christmas decorations still on full display. Although the holiday season had been over for several weeks, the town had clearly decided to keep the celebration going.

Isabelle felt a smile twitching at both sides of her lips. There was something so endearing about the sentimentality of prolonging the celebratory season. She loved Christmas. She had chosen to postpone her relocation so she could have one last holiday with her family. It had been beautiful and heartwarming and achingly sad at the same time. But she wouldn't trade it for anything in the world. She would hold on to those memories for the rest of her life.

She slowed down as a gold and cream sign caught her attention. *North Star Chocolate Shop*. It was her new place of employment. The company, North Star Chocolate, was a well-known chocolatier and famous for creating exceptional chocolates. Although she couldn't see inside the place, the exterior was inviting. In the storefront window sat a display of confections that tempted her sweet tooth. Brightly colored teapots accompanied them. She was really going to have to resist the temptation to sample every morsel of chocolate in the shop. As she continued driving down Main Street, a fantastic aroma began to filter into the truck. Suddenly a pink neon sign came into view that explained the smell. The Snowy Owl Diner.

The establishment looked so pretty set against the white snow and the mountains. She couldn't remember the last time she'd eaten at an old-fashioned diner. It had to be over a decade ago, at the one back home in Miami. Her family had frequented the place when she was little. Eating there had always been an adventure.

On impulse, Isabelle drove into the lot and made her way to the entrance. Her stomach was grumbling fiercely. The nervousness she'd felt all morning had made eating breakfast impossible. Now she was starving. Nothing less would have prompted her to stop in at the establishment way before she considered herself ready to be in any social setting. Determined not to change her mind, she pushed open the door with extra force, her head held high. She heard a loud thump followed by a cry and a crashing sound. Within seconds she realized the door had hit someone.

She stood in the doorway, horror-struck at the sight that greeted her. A man was on the floor surrounded by a sticky substance that looked an awful lot like syrup amid broken pieces of ceramic. All eyes in the diner were focused on her and the unfortunate man.

Isabelle's heart sank. Her instructions had been to blend into the fabric of Owl Creek without attracting any attention to herself. Yet her first foray into the heart of town had resulted in garnering way more attention than she wanted or needed. Although her very first instinct was to turn tail and run as far away from the Snowy Owl Diner as her legs would carry her, it was far too late to do so.

*　*　*

Connor North had frantically tried to save himself from falling, but once the syrup spilled, his heel slid on the sticky parquet floor and he'd landed with a thud on his backside. Pain sliced through him, and he let out a loud groan.

"Oh, no! I'm so sorry! Are you all right?"

He looked up at the sound of the soft, melodic voice inquiring about his well-being. The woman he was staring up at was definitely not a resident of Owl Creek. He would have noticed a woman this beautiful before now. Jet-black hair fell around her shoulders in soft waves. Her sweet brown eyes radiated compassion. Thick, soot-colored lashes framed them.

He wondered what she was doing in town. Perhaps another tourist eager to experience North Star Chocolates and a quaint village in Alaska.

Connor sprang to his feet, wincing at the sticky sensation on his hands. He brushed them against his sweater to clean them off.

"No need to worry. I'm fine. I'm Connor North. And you are?" he asked, holding out his hand so she could shake it.

She gazed at him with wide eyes. Her mouth opened, but no words came out. She looked down at his hand with a blank stare. "I… I'm Ella. Ella Perez. I'm so very sorry for making such a mess." He withdrew his hand when she didn't shake it.

"You're forgiven, Ella. Accidents happen," Connor said with a nod, trying to put the stranger at ease. She was gazing at him with a look of trepidation. Had he done something to alarm her? Maybe she thought he was upset about the fall.

"Is everything all right over here?"

Connor swung his gaze toward Piper Miller, the owner of the Snowy Owl

Diner. Piper was the town's resident sweetheart, as well as his younger brother Braden's fiancée.

"It's fine, Piper," Connor said, making a face and looking down at his soggy pants. "I just had a clumsy moment. Sorry about the mess." He pointed toward the syrup and broken dish on the parquet floor.

"No worries," Piper said. "We're used to spills around here. I'll have it cleaned up right away."

"He's being kind," Ella interjected. "I swung the door too hard when I came inside and it crashed into him. I'm so sorry for the trouble." Regret rang out in her voice. "It was entirely my fault."

"You must be new in town if you think that's trouble," Piper responded. "I'm the owner of this place by the way. Piper Miller."

"Ella Perez. I… I've just moved to Owl Creek," she explained, running a shaky hand through her long dark tresses. Connor was trying not to stare, but he couldn't seem to help himself. Ella Perez was without a doubt the prettiest woman who'd ever stepped foot in Owl Creek.

"Let me show you to a table." Piper looked back and forth between them. "Unless the two of you are sitting together?"

"No! We're not together," Ella said in an emphatic tone that brooked no argument. "I just need a table for one."

"That can be arranged," Piper said. "Follow me and I'll get you situated. Connor, why don't you go over to the counter and grab some more syrup?"

"Nice to meet you," Connor said with a nod as Piper led Ella to a table by the window. He grabbed another container of syrup from the counter and headed back to eat his breakfast.

His two best friends, Gabriel Lawson and Hank Crawford, were seated at their regular table waiting for him to bring the syrup back. When he reached the table he could see the two of them trying to stifle their laughter.

Connor placed the syrup down on the table with a bang. "As you saw, I took one for the team by going to get this."

"And we're mighty appreciative of your service," Hank said with a smirk. He reached over and picked up the container, pouring the syrup liberally over his flapjacks.

Hank handed the syrup to Gabriel, who did the same. "Looks like you made a new friend." Gabriel wiggled his eyebrows. Connor pretended not to notice. Anytime he was within a ten-mile radius of a single woman, his best friends couldn't resist teasing him about his prolific dating history. Lately it had been bugging him.

Although Connor's stomach was growling and he had a full breakfast plate sitting before him, something was bothering him. He knew he'd never met

Ella before, but her name pricked at him. Why did it sound so familiar?

He stroked his jaw. "I can't put my finger on it, but I feel like I know her name for some reason. Ella Perez. Does it sound familiar to either one of you?" he asked, trying to recall why the woman's name lurked in the back of his mind.

Gabriel and Hank exchanged a pointed glance. Both of them began to chuckle as if they were sharing an inside joke.

Connor let out a sigh. "What are you guys laughing at now?"

"It's just that you make it a point to know every pretty woman in Owl Creek, even the tourists," Gabriel explained.

"Neither her name nor her face ring a bell with me," Hank added, still chuckling. "But then again, I'm a happily married man."

The laughter erupting from their

mouths threatened to drown out all of his thoughts. Couldn't he even talk to a woman without people assuming he was interested in her? Sure, Ella was stunning, but it didn't mean he wanted to date her.

Normally, Connor didn't mind being teased about his love life, but lately it had rankled him every time Hank and Gabriel joked about his status as Owl Creek's most popular bachelor. He didn't know why it bothered him so much as of late, but it was beginning to get old. He wasn't the same man he'd been a year ago. Connor had grown and matured.

So much had changed in the last year with the return of his long-lost sister, Sage. She had been kidnapped as a baby from their family home in Owl Creek, only to return to the fold twenty-five years later. The reunion had also brought his brother, Braden, back to town, making the family unit complete. Although he should have been on solid ground, he'd been feeling unsettled. His best friends were both newlyweds—Hank had married Sage, while Gabriel had reunited with his first love, Rachel. Even Braden had fallen in love with Piper, his best friend since childhood.

Everyone seemed to be moving forward in their lives, except him.

"Hey! We're just having a little fun," Hank said, clapping him on the shoulder. "What's troubling you?"

Connor stabbed his fork on the plate and picked up several pieces of pancake. He shrugged as he stuffed the forkful in his mouth, then swallowed. "I don't know, guys. I'm just feeling a bit out of sorts these days. Things have been pretty intense lately. I think it's all beginning to catch up with me."

"They really have been," Gabriel agreed. "Personally speaking, the past few months have been a whirlwind. Ra-

chel and I are married now and raising twin toddlers." He grinned. "God
blessed me when I least expected it."

"You deserve every ounce of happiness," Connor said, raising his glass of
orange juice in Gabe's direction.

"We're here for you, Connor. You
know that. The Three Amigos for life."
Hank held up his hand and bumped fists
with him.

Connor grinned. Having his two closest friends in his corner always made
him feel as if he could conquer the
world. And since Braden had recently
decided to forgo working at the family business, the North Star Chocolate
Company, he would need all that confidence and determination to ensure the
company's success. Not that he held it
against his younger brother. He admired
Braden's desire to live life on his own
terms. He had the type of courage Connor wasn't sure he himself had.

For the next half hour Connor and his

friends ate and talked, focusing on local matters in Owl Creek. As town sheriff, Hank always had his ear to the ground. A few times Connor found himself looking across the diner at Ella as she ate her meal. He was curious as to what she was doing here in town.

She'd casually mentioned being a new resident in their small village, but he wondered if she had family or friends here. Had she relocated for a romantic connection? In these parts it was entirely possible. Or perhaps she'd come here for an employment opportunity.

A job! His family's chocolate emporium. That's why her name sounded so familiar. Ella Perez was the new manager at the North Star Chocolate Shop right down the street. He'd seen her résumé and offer letter just the other day on his grandmother Beulah's desk.

When he glanced back over in Ella's direction, she was sailing out the front door.

He reached into his pocket, pulled out

some bills, then plunked them down on the table. "Spending time with you guys was a pleasure, but I have to settle some work-related business," he said, standing up and pulling on his parka. "Breakfast is on me."

Before Gabe or Hank could say a word, Connor hustled toward the exit. If he moved really quickly, perhaps he could catch up to Ella and introduce himself as a member of the North family and welcome her to town.

He immediately spotted her heading toward the parking lot. "Ella!" he called out in a raised voice. When she didn't turn around, Connor called her name in an even louder voice. When she didn't respond, he picked up the pace, closing the distance between them in a few quick strides. Although he continued to call out her name, she didn't turn around.

In a last ditch effort to get her attention, he tapped her on the shoulder. Ella whipped around to face him, a look of pure terror etched on her face. Her entire body had stiffened up.

"Hey. I didn't mean to scare you," he said, immediately regretting touching her. He didn't think he'd crossed a boundary, but perhaps he had unknowingly done so.

"You didn't," she said, her voice trembling. "You just caught me off guard."

"Sorry about that, but I had to catch up to you before you left. When we met I couldn't help but think you seemed familiar to me. And I know exactly who you are, Ella Perez."

Chapter Two

Isabelle felt frozen in place. Her hands began to break out in a sweat. A wild rhythm began to beat in her chest. A huge lump sat in her throat, making speaking impossible. How on earth had Connor figured out her identity? She'd barely been in town for twenty-four hours. Jonah had assured her that her identity would be secure in Owl Creek as long as she abided by the rules. To her knowledge, she hadn't broken a single one. How could things have fallen apart so fast? Now she would have to leave this Alaskan village and plant roots somewhere else.

"You know who I am?" she asked, her voice sounding raspy.

Connor nodded as a grin slowly stretched across his face, making him appear even more handsome than she'd initially thought. "You're the new hire for my family's chocolate shop. If I remember correctly, you're starting this week."

She felt her entire body sag in relief. *Phew.* Due to her nerves, she'd completely misread the situation. Her status in WITSEC wasn't in jeopardy after all.

"I guess I should have picked up on your last name," Isabelle said. She'd been so nervous after she'd caused him to fall that she hadn't made the connection between him and the North Star Chocolate Company. "My start date is tomorrow actually. I'm really grateful for the opportunity."

"Welcome to Owl Creek, Ella. I think

you're going to love our little part of Alaska. I know I'm biased, but it's a fantastic place to live."

"Well, it's unlike anything I've ever known. Florida never sees snow. There's a whole lot I'm going to have to get accustomed to, particularly the climate." A feeling of dread washed over her. She'd just said Florida out of habit. How had she slipped up so early on? "I meant to say Flagstaff not Florida. Though I've spent many summers in the Sunshine State," she quickly added, praying Connor hadn't noticed anything strange about her statement. Even though she'd practiced reciting her backstory with Jonah a hundred times or more, clearly it hadn't stuck.

"What made you apply for a job so far from home?" he asked, his brows knitted together.

Her heart began to hammer in her chest. Was he suspicious of her or simply asking normal questions? It was hard not to feel paranoid under the circumstances.

What would Connor North think if she told him the truth? That she'd chosen to rebuild her life in Alaska because it was far away from the danger she faced in Miami. Planting herself in a remote Alaskan town had been about survival. She'd made the hardest decision in her life by leaving everything she held dear in her rearview mirror. As a result, her heart had been completely shattered.

She shifted from one foot to the other. "I needed a change of pace," she said instead. "Owl Creek seemed like it would do the trick."

"That was mighty brave of you. Alaska isn't for the faint of heart, especially when you're used to a warmer climate."

Isabelle nodded. "I also happen to really love chocolate, so I'm excited about working for North Star Chocolate. So far I've been communicating with Beulah. She's been incredible. And very kind."

Connor grinned. "That's my grandmother. She's can be quite a character, but she always leads with her heart."

His grandmother. Her heart ached for her own sweet-faced *avo.* Carmen Sanchez was the most loving woman in the world. She'd helped to raise Isabelle. It was near impossible to imagine not being in her grandmother's presence. Due to her grandmother's serious medical condition, Isabelle had no expectation of ever seeing her again. Her eyes felt moist, and she knew she needed to get in the car before she started crying in front of Connor. That would certainly raise a red flag.

"Well, thanks for the warm welcome. I should head back to the house. I'm still getting settled in." She tried to inject positivity into her tone, even though the reality of her situation had just crashed over her with full force. Nothing would ever be the same.

"Enjoy the rest of your day. Before you know it, you'll be able to navigate Owl Creek like a pro."

With a lame wave, Isabelle turned toward her new vehicle and slid into the driver's seat. She turned the car on and let the engine warm up a little before she headed away from Main Street and toward the northern part of town. Although she felt the urge to turn back and get one last look at Connor, she knew it wouldn't be wise to take her gaze away from the snow-packed road. She wasn't used to driving in these conditions, and she needed to focus all of her attention on the road.

With his dark hair, blue eyes and rugged frame, Connor North was gorgeous. He radiated an air of confidence. At the moment she could use a dose of it to bolster her frame of mind. Even in syrup-stained pants, he'd walked around the diner as if he owned it. There was no harm in looking at an attractive man, she reminded herself. Though anything more was out of the question. How could she ever start a relationship knowing her entire life was a lie? The rules of WITSEC forbade her from ever telling a romantic partner the truth about her existence.

She refused to go down that road. It was hard enough making everyone in Owl Creek think she was someone she wasn't. Adding in romance would be disastrous.

Connor watched as Ella headed off in the direction of her new digs. A strange feeling had settled over him during his conversation with North Star Chocolate's newest hire. He couldn't fathom why he felt it so intensely, but Connor knew instinctively she wasn't as she appeared to be. This beautiful newcomer to town was running from something.

He had no idea what it was—a divorce, a bad relationship, a fractured family? Perhaps she was a criminal. The possibilities were endless. As they'd spoken, there had been something radiating from her that didn't ring true. Just now she'd mentioned Florida, then corrected herself to say Flagstaff. And she hadn't responded when he'd called out her name. He didn't think he was imagining things either. Connor knew he was more jaded than most people, but he trusted his instincts. He'd grown up in a household that had never recovered from the trauma of his baby sister's abduction at three months old. As a result, Connor had been mistrustful of people, particularly tourists and newcomers to Owl Creek.

Ella Perez was raising all of his hackles. Her stunning looks hadn't rendered him incapable of picking up on certain cues she'd emitted. She'd acted nervous, as if she was on edge about something.

What if she was up to no good here in town? He let himself into his vehicle, chiding himself for not asking more probing questions.

The newcomer seemed out of place in a town like Owl Creek. Why had a woman like Ella come all the way to Alaska for a job at his family's company? Alaska was at times a harsh and unforgiving land. For a man who considered himself to be pragmatic, it didn't make a lot of sense.

Connor let out a sigh and rested his head against the steering wheel. His paranoia was rising to the surface and threatening to choke him. He tended to believe the worst of people based on his family's past trauma. Although he tried to control his suspicious nature, Connor didn't trust strangers. He always felt as if he was waiting for them to peel back the mask and reveal their true selves.

In all likelihood, Ella was a sweet young woman who was merely nervous about starting a brand-new job in a world completely unfamiliar to her. Guilt sliced through him. He wasn't being fair to her or himself. He needed to let go of the past and accept people at face value. Being so cynical wasn't a good quality. As a man of faith, he knew it wasn't right to judge others so harshly. But he still couldn't quiet the voice inside him warning him against accepting Ella at face value.

By the time he reached the chocolate factory, Connor was ready to focus on something other than the mysterious new resident of Owl Creek. He enjoyed working at his family's company. As an executive in charge of distribution and product development, he had helped the company grow and expand its reach in key markets over the last five years. He also oversaw the operation of the Owl Creek factory and served as the CEO's right-hand man. Thankfully, Beulah was the CEO, and he adored collaborating with her.

The aroma of chocolate permeated the air as he walked inside. Every morning before he made his way to his office Connor enjoyed strolling through the factory where the chocolate was being made. He liked talking with the employees and even helping out on the conveyer belt. When they were kids, he and Braden had gotten a thrill out of plucking chocolate confections from the assembly line and popping them into their mouths. More times than not it had resulted in a competition between them. Trying to consume chocolate the fastest had always led to bellyaches and admonishments from Beulah.

"Chocolate is to be savored, not devoured." Just the thought of his grandmother uttering those words to the pint-size version of himself made him chuckle out loud. Beulah had always been a fountain of wisdom. Nothing much had changed in that regard. His grandmother was still a unique woman who continued to fascinate him.

The factory had been his and Braden's stomping grounds—they'd learned the business as they played and explored in the chocolate factory. Despite the tragedy involving the abduction of their sister, there had been an abundance of joy in their lives. Of course there had been sorrow as well. None of them had ever fully recovered from the loss until Sage's recent return to the fold. Now he should be completely over it, but he wasn't. He still harbored a lot of anger. The woman who'd abducted his sister had been visiting town as one of the leaders of a youth group. No one had ever suspected her of wrongdoing or been suspicious of her actions. Over the years, people had sought to take advantage of his family by pretending to have information about his sister's whereabouts. A few women had even presented themselves as the missing North family member, which had only added to their pain. It showed him that people couldn't always be trusted. A person always had to be on guard.

"Good morning, my dear. How was your breakfast with the boys?" Beulah's voice rang out as he walked toward the executive offices. When he turned around, his grandmother was walking toward him with the vigor of someone half her age. As always, Beulah North was dressed in a suit jacket and matching skirt, with her signature pearls draped around her neck. She believed in dressing to impress as the CEO of the North Star Chocolate Company.

Connor pressed a kiss on her cheek after she caught up to him. "Morning. It was delicious. And I just met our new hire at the diner."

"Which one? We've hired several in the past few weeks."

"Ella Perez," he said.

"Oh, yes. She starts tomorrow at the chocolate shop. I'm going to be there to greet her in the morning. What was your impression? Her résumé and telephone interview were impressive."

Connor hesitated a moment before speaking. He didn't want Beulah to think he was being hard on their new hire. "Are you sure she's right for the job? There was something about her that didn't really gel with Owl Creek or the manager position."

Beulah frowned at him. "Whatever do you mean?"

Connor shrugged. "I don't know. She fumbled a bit when we were talking. I'm not sure how to explain it without sounding paranoid, but I just got the feeling she wasn't being fully transparent. It was like she was hiding something."

Beulah stared at him without speaking. Her eyes began to blink like an owl, which served as a sure sign that his grandmother was gathering her words. "You've just met her, Connor. Why don't you extend her a measure of grace rather than being suspicious?" She reached out and touched his cheek. "You have to stop focusing on the worst parts of humanity, especially since there are so many good people in the world. What happened to our family all those years ago was horrific, but God brought our sweet girl home so we could heal. I'm worried you're still stuck in the past, Connor."

His grandmother's words served as a punch to his gut. He hated the notion that he was stuck in the past, especially since everyone else seemed to be doing fine. Connor had tried to find closure with Sage's return to Owl Creek, but he still harbored feelings of resentment for all the years that had been stolen from them.

"I'll try to do better," he vowed, wishing the words resonated more within him. He felt a sense of powerlessness. Connor knew he hadn't been able to conquer this issue no matter how hard he'd tried. But he couldn't admit that to his grandmother. She was counting on him to be the future of the chocolate company.

"That's all I'll ever ask of you," Beulah said, tears pooling in her eyes. "I count on you more than you realize. You're my North Star. No pun intended," she said, letting out a cackle. The corners of her eyes crinkled up.

Leave it to Beulah to make him laugh when two seconds ago he'd been feeling badly about himself. She was an incredible woman. He wished that he could be as resilient as Beulah. She was the strongest member of their family.

Connor looked at his watch. "I'm going to get prepped for our meeting with the distributors."

"Good idea. I'll see you in the conference room. I can't wait to taste the new white chocolate hot cocoa." Beulah rubbed her hands together and grinned. As the driving force behind the company, she still felt enthusiastic about her work. It was one of the main reasons for the success of North Star Chocolates. Passion combined with heartfelt dedication.

"I think we might have another hit on our hands," Connor drawled, feeling proud of the collaboration between himself, Sage and Braden. Creating new products was one of the best aspects of his job. Working with his siblings on this special project had been so much fun, particularly since it rarely happened. It had almost made up for the fact that Braden wouldn't be working alongside him at the company. It was reassuring to know their bond was still tight.

Connor made his way to his office. Just looking around the room made him grin. He'd decorated it with a fun vibe in mind. Since he spent so much time at work, he'd wanted it to be comfortable yet functional. The bubble gum machine served as a colorful reminder that he was still a kid at heart.

Connor sat down at his desk and logged on to his computer. Even though he was trying to focus on the upcoming meeting, thoughts of the mysterious newcomer refused to completely fade away. There was something about her that caused curiosity to well up inside him. Although he knew his grandmother had given him sound advice, he couldn't stop wondering about Ella Perez.

He imagined she knew very little about Alaskan living. He had only been to Arizona a few times on business, but it was clear to him how vastly different it was from Owl Creek. He couldn't imagine it would be easy for Ella to get her bearings while navigating a new job. She didn't know a soul here in town and she'd probably left family and friends behind in Arizona. As a hometown boy, Connor had only left Owl Creek in order to attend college in Anchorage. Unlike Ella, he'd only been a short flight away from home and his loved ones.

A feeling of shame seized him. Instead of harboring suspicions about Ella, he should be wholeheartedly welcoming her to the North Star Chocolate fold. He should be trying to help her get acclimated. In a perfect world he would be more like his grandmother. He let out a ragged sigh. The truth nagged at him. He hadn't healed from his family's trauma, and he wasn't sure he ever would.

Isabelle let out a huge sigh of relief as she turned off Route 65. She had driven by the turnoff several times without realizing she should have taken the right turn rather than continuing straight ahead. Seeing a Moose Crossing sign a few miles back had caused her adrenaline to race. She had immediately slowed down to five miles an hour out of an abundance of caution. Thankfully her new home wasn't too far from town. If she hadn't gotten confused with the GPS directions, it would have only been a ten-minute ride. At least she didn't have to travel too far to reach her place of employment.

When she pulled up to 10 Kodiak Lane, she felt a huge sense of relief at being safely home.

Home. She felt a little hitch in her heart at the notion that this quaint little abode now belonged to her. Once she made her way inside the house, Isabelle sank down onto the sofa and pressed her eyes shut. Her temple was pounding with a tension headache. Everything was beginning to weigh her down. Tomorrow was her niece's second birthday, and she'd be missing the special celebration. It was breaking Isabelle's heart knowing she would miss all of Celia's birthdays and special occasions from this point forward. Celia would grow up without knowing Isabelle. Her sister, Denise, was her best friend and closest confidante. Who would she go to the movies with? Who would wish her a happy birthday? Or cheer for her when she experienced a triumph?

Tears slid down her face as a feeling of hopelessness swept over her. In the morning she would have to report to work at the North Star Chocolate Shop and put on a brave face. It would be a huge step in the development of her new identity. But she didn't feel courageous or strong in the slightest bit. Isabelle felt as if she might crack into a million little pieces at any given moment. And sadly, if she did, there wouldn't be anyone who cared enough about her to pick up the pieces.

Chapter Three

Morning came well before Isabelle was ready to leave the coziness of her down comforter and heated blanket. She let out a groan as her alarm blared, putting an end to her peaceful slumber. She'd been a little chilly last night and she'd rummaged around in the hall closet looking for bedding since she couldn't locate the thermostat in the furnished rental. Her footed pajamas, along with the comfy blankets, made her feel as if she was snuggled in a cocoon and she was reluctant to get up.

After dragging herself out of bed, Isabelle fixed herself some oatmeal and coffee before heading back upstairs to wash up and get dressed. She looked at herself in the bathroom mirror. She'd pulled her long black hair back into a ponytail. She was only wearing a light dusting of concealer and mascara. In her black sweater and matching slacks, she looked competent and professional. Isabelle took a deep breath and began to recite her daily mantra.

"You cannot go home. You cannot contact anyone from your former life. Don't do anything to raise suspicions. If you follow the rules, you'll be safe."

Just saying the words out loud felt surreal. She felt like one of those hapless women from a TV movie. How on earth had her life spiraled out of control so quickly? The last few months had been a living nightmare with each day bleaker than the last. It had been bad enough to witness a brutal crime, but things had taken a turn for the worse once the authorities asked her to provide testimony against Burke, who'd put a hit out on her. Several harrowing attempts had been made on her life. Although each one had been unsuccessful, the fear escalated with each attempt.

She shook her head, willing herself not to go down this road. Today was her first workday in Owl Creek. A rush of adrenaline raced through her. It reminded her of the way she'd felt on the first day of school—nervous mixed with excited. In order to maintain her sanity, she needed to embrace everything Owl Creek had to offer. Moping around wouldn't serve any purpose other than to dampen her spirits even further. She needed to stay hopeful and grounded in her new reality. Her life wasn't over, even though it sometimes felt like it. Maybe she would fall in love with her managerial position at the chocolate shop. Perhaps Owl Creek would be an answer to all of her most fervent prayers. She yearned to feel safe, despite the fact that she'd had to move so far away from home and sever all ties with her former life in order to make it happen. Suddenly, she was second-guessing herself. Had she made the right choice in entering WITSEC? Maybe she'd allowed fear to guide her decision.

Lord, please help me to have a positive outlook as I take these first few steps in Owl Creek. I'm so frightened, and I feel so alone. I've never been without my family. Help me navigate my way through the darkness.

As she drove toward town, Isabelle made sure she traversed the roads carefully. Driving over snow-packed roads wasn't for the faint of heart as she was beginning to realize from firsthand experience. She gripped the steering wheel tightly as the tires slid over an icy patch. Her nerves were on edge.

You can do this. Her mother's voice

buzzed in her ear, enveloping her like a warm embrace. Isabelle missed her more than she could ever express in words. Though the Sanchez family had never had much in the way of material things, Mama had always given her children wings and allowed them to soar. The thought of never seeing Mama again or hearing the lilting tone of her voice gutted her. Hot tears pooled in her eyes.

Do not cry! she urged herself. Today was not the day to break down. She needed to establish herself in this town and get her bearings in her place of employment. Despite her stomach being tied up in knots, Isabelle had to project an air of composure. It was going to be way harder than she had ever imagined. This was where her faith would be more important to her than ever.

"'I can do all things through Christ which strengtheneth me,'" Isabelle said, reciting the verse from Philippians as a calming mechanism. She often drew from Bible passages in troubled times. This one was no different.

By the time the shops on Main Street came into view, she had managed to collect herself. The white chalet-style shop looked even more charming this morning. She pulled into the back lot as she'd been instructed and parked. Walking inside the North Star Chocolate Shop felt like stepping into a whole new world. The interior was done in shades of gold and cream with splashes of brown and pink. A small chandelier hung above a display case that was a chocolate lover's dream. The aroma filled her nostrils, and she felt a heady sensation to be surrounded by so much chocolate.

"Good morning. You must be Ella!" A very distinguished-looking woman greeted her from behind the counter. With her jet-black hair streaked with silver and a widow's peak, the woman had a striking appearance. "I'm Beulah North," she said, sticking out her hand in greeting as she moved toward Isabelle.

Isabelle reached out and shook hands with her new boss. "Yes, I'm Ella Perez. It's great to meet you in person, Mrs. North, after all of our phone conversations."

"It's a pleasure to meet you face-to-face. You're lovely," Beulah crowed. "We're mighty pleased to have you here in Owl Creek. Welcome to the North Star Chocolate family. And I'll be offended if you don't call me Beulah."

Something about this dazzling woman made her smile. She couldn't put her finger on it, but she just knew they were going to be fast friends. "I'm happy to be here, Beulah."

"This is my granddaughter, Sage Crawford," Beulah said, turning toward the younger woman by her side.

Sage was beautiful in a girl-next-door

kind of way. She radiated happiness. Sage smiled at Isabelle, and said, "Hi, Ella. We're so happy you'll be working with us. I just know you're going to love being here."

Isabelle waved her hand around the area. "What's not to love? This place is fantastic. Every chocolate lover's dream. If the chocolate is even half as good as it smells, I'll be delighted."

"Oh, our chocolate is divine," Beulah crowed. "I'll make sure to give you plenty of samples to take home with you tonight. Then you can tell us your favorites."

"That sounds like a great homework assignment," Isabelle said, garnering laughter from Sage and Beulah.

"Why don't we give you the grand tour?" Sage suggested. Isabelle nodded, then followed behind the women as they led her around. Although she had worked in retail spaces before such as coffeehouses, clothing shops and bookstores, Isabelle had never been employed by a company the caliber of North Star Chocolate. Everywhere she looked were examples of excellence. Awards of distinction were framed on the wall. The display cases were filled with so many assortments of chocolates—Belgian chocolates, pecan clusters, chocolate-covered raisins, truffles, nonpareils and so many more, many of which she'd never heard of before.

Although her head was spinning with all the details, she was beginning to feel enthused about working at the chocolate shop. She knew she had a lot to learn about the company, and as manager, she would be in charge of the store as well as its employees. Once Sage and Beulah finished showing her around and introduced her to the employees, they sat down in the café portion of the shop and enjoyed cups of North Star's signature hot chocolate.

"You weren't exaggerating when you

raved about the hot cocoa," Isabelle said after taking several sips of the delicious treat.

"Thank you. I'd tell you the secret ingredient but it's a North family secret," Beulah said, winking at her. Her eyes twinkled with delight. Isabelle had the feeling Beulah North was a unique individual with many different facets to her.

Isabelle chuckled. "I don't blame you one bit. The recipe is pure gold."

"Speaking of family, what does yours think about this move to Alaska?" Sage asked, a hint of curiosity in her tone.

Isabelle's mind went blank. What could she say? That her family was devastated by her decision to enter WITSEC? Should she explain that the minimal risks to her family members' lives hadn't justified their participation in the program?

"I don't have much family to speak of," she answered. She felt awful for denying the existence of her large, bustling family, but it would be better in the long run so it wouldn't look strange not to mention them. Cutting her family out of her past, present and future was her new reality.

Beulah made a tutting sound. "I'm sorry to hear that, but in a town like Owl Creek, it won't be long before you'll be considered as one of our own."

Sage flashed a wide grin. "I can attest to that!"

"Well, I hate to drink and run, but I need to head over to the factory for a meeting. Sage will stay with you and show you the ropes," Beulah explained. "We'll have to get you over there one day this week. I'd love for you to meet the team and see how the chocolate is created and assembled. Even after all these years I find it fascinating."

Isabelle didn't dare tell Beulah that she'd already met her grandson. She still felt mortified about being responsible for Connor's fall. The very last thing she wanted to do was cause Beulah to think badly of her. Maybe in the future she would look back on the incident and find it hysterically funny, but at the moment it was humiliating.

Way to make a wonderful first impression on her boss's family, she scolded herself. She wouldn't blame Connor if he was questioning why Beulah had hired her in the first place. Although he'd treated her with an abundance of kindness yesterday, Isabelle knew he had just been doing his job as the company's ambassador.

A man like Connor North had the world in the palm of his hand. He was good-looking, charming and one of the heirs to a chocolate empire. She imagined he had his fair share of admirers. He was what her mother called a catch. If the situation was different, Isabelle wouldn't mind getting to know him better. But it simply wasn't possible. Any type of relationship—whether a casual

flirtation or something more meaningful—was off the table. It wouldn't be
fair to get close to someone and have
to lie to them about the most important
parts of herself.

According to the rules of WITSEC,
she could never divulge her former
identity to anyone, not even her future
spouse. As a result, Isabelle knew she
would never settle down or have children. It was hard enough having to live
a life filled with so many fabrications,
but she refused to drag anyone else
into the mess. She'd grown up watching her parents enjoy a marriage based
on mutual trust and admiration. They
were best friends and partners who finished each other's sentences. And she
couldn't imagine either one harboring
secrets from the other. To this day they
were completely in love with each other.
They even had weekly date nights that
they never missed. Ana and Rio Sanchez were her romantic ideals.

If she couldn't aspire to that type of partnership—where truth reigned supreme—then she didn't intend to have one at all. Not ever.

Connor had a million things to do at work, but somehow he'd ended up on Main Street standing in front of the North Star Chocolate Shop. It was only one block away from the chocolate factory where he worked, so it had been a simple walk to get over here. The shop was a great draw for both the townsfolk and tourists, while the factory was where all the confections were made and packaged.

Just the sight of the store made him grin. His first job had been working the register after school. It had taught him about discipline, hard work and his family's legacy. And even though he'd loved chocolate since he came out of the womb, he had fallen in love with it all over again. Seeing the joy it brought to customers had been a life-changing experience. He'd known at that moment that he didn't want to do anything other than work for the North Star Chocolate Company for the rest of his life.

Curiosity about Beulah's new hire had been nipping at his mind all morning long. Was Ella enjoying working at the chocolate shop? Was she feeling at all overwhelmed about settling down in a small Alaskan town? He couldn't help but wonder if she would stay in Owl Creek. Occasionally, newcomers who weren't used to the harsh weather and the Alaskan way of life had packed up and left without giving Owl Creek a fair chance.

He pushed the shop door open and inhaled the sweet scent that was as familiar to him as his own name. Being here felt like going back to his roots. The sights, smells and sounds were awakening all of his senses. It made him smile to see so many townsfolk milling about the shop, excited about picking out their favorite chocolates. He immediately spotted Ella standing behind the counter with his sister. The two women were chatting amiably as if they'd known each other for years.

"Good afternoon, ladies," Connor said as he walked toward them.

Although he tried not to stare, he couldn't seem to look away from Ella. With her hair swept away from her face, her stunning features were on full display. Her attire was professional and stylish. She looked right at home in the shop.

"Hey, Connor. What brings you over here?" Sage asked. "Are you checking up on me?"

Before he could answer, she continued speaking. "Ella, this is my brother, Connor North. Connor, this is Ella Perez, our new store manager."

"We've already met," Connor said, the corners of his mouth twitching in amusement at the memory of their first meeting at the Snowy Owl.

"At the diner," Ella said as she shot him a pointed look. Clearly, she didn't want Sage to know about the incident with the syrup. He sent her a slight nod, letting her know her secret was safe with him. He didn't want to do anything to make her uncomfortable. As it was, he felt pretty guilty about telling his grandmother she might be concealing something. He knew he had to make it up to Ella in some way for doubting her authenticity.

"I'm glad you stumbled upon the Snowy Owl," Sage said. "My sister-in-law, Piper, is the owner, and she makes the best flapjacks in the state of Alaska."

"I'll remember that for next time," Ella said, grinning.

"So, how are things going?" he asked. "I hope your first day has been enjoyable."

"It's going very well," she answered, looking at Sage for confirmation. "Your sister and grandmother really rolled out the welcome mat for me. I couldn't have asked for more on my first day."

"We're so glad you're here," Sage said, placing her arm around Ella. "Can you just excuse me for a moment? The mother of one of my students just walked in. I'd like to say hello."

"Students?" Ella asked, furrowing her brow as Sage hustled away.

"Sage is a part-time teacher. Her teaching schedule allows her to help out here and at the factory a few days a week," Connor explained.

Ella nodded. "I imagine she's a wonderful teacher. She's been so patient with me today."

Connor had no way of knowing if Ella knew his sister's backstory. It had been front-page news when it had been revealed that the long-lost chocolate heiress had returned to Owl Creek. There was nothing in Ella's expression or voice that hinted at anything other than pure admiration for Sage. As far as he was concerned, his little sister was the most resilient, loving person he'd ever known.

"So, did Beulah pick out some chocolates for you to take home?" he asked, knowing it was his grandmother's signature gesture she extended to new employees. Chocolate was Beulah's love language, and she didn't hesitate to shower people with it.

"She did. She asked me what my favorites were, and I told her that I love it all. I'm not sure how a person can have an absolute favorite."

Connor felt his eyes widening. He let out a sharp laugh.

"Did I say something funny?" Ella asked with a slight frown.

"I'm sorry," Connor said, his tone apologetic. "I didn't mean to be rude. Let me show you something." Connor walked behind the counter and opened the display case. He scanned the rows of chocolates, homing in on several before he picked them up and placed them on a napkin. He turned toward Ella and pointed toward the chocolates. "These three chocolates are my all-time favorites. This one here is the purest milk chocolate. I fell in love with it when I was eight years old." He broke the confection in half and handed it to Ella, who gingerly bit into it. "Now this one here is a chocolate truffle. When I was eighteen, you couldn't tell me there was a finer chocolate." Once again he split the chocolate in half. He watched as Ella eagerly popped it into her mouth.

"Oh, this is delicious," she said, letting out a contented sigh. "So when did you fall in love with the third one?"

Connor held up the piece of white chocolate. "This one has only been a recent discovery. I spent most of my life thinking white chocolate just wasn't on the same level as regular chocolate. At the advanced age of twenty-seven I fell head over heels in love with white chocolate." Connor dramatically snapped the piece of white chocolate in half and handed Ella one as he bit into his own portion.

"Sounds like a serious relationship," she said with a chuckle. The sound of Ella's tinkling laughter warmed his insides. She seemed more relaxed today. He was beginning to see glimpses of her personality shining through her reserve.

They were standing so close to one another their arms were brushing against each other. A slight awareness flared between them seconds before Ella moved a few steps away from him. A shuttered expression came over her face and he had the distinct impression his close proximity had made her uncomfortable. At the moment, Ella was giving off signs he rarely encountered.

Connor was used to being playful and friendly with the women in Owl Creek. In fact, he had gained a reputation of being a ladies' man. Just because he'd always had a healthy dating life didn't mean he was a player. And even if he had been at one point, wasn't he allowed to evolve?

Suddenly, a bang emanated from outside, echoing in the shop.

Ella let out a scream as her features creased with fear. For a moment Connor was struck by the sheer terror on her face.

"There's nothing to be afraid of," Connor said, instinctively moving toward her and placing his arm around her. All of his protective instincts had gone into high gear.

"W-what was that sound?" she asked, her eyes wide, lips trembling.

Connor strode toward the window and peered outside. In a matter of seconds, he turned back toward her. "It was just a truck backfiring."

"Otis's truck? Not again! He really needs to get that thing fixed," Sage called out from across the store. She shook her head and made a face.

"I'm so embarrassed," Ella said, ducking her head. Her body was still shaking.

"Hey. It's nothing to feel badly about. You should see me during a thunderstorm," Connor said, trying to ease the tension.

Ella sent him a smile that didn't make it all the way to her eyes. One moment everything had been fine, and the next she'd been falling apart. It didn't make any sense. Was she the high-strung type?

"Is everything okay over here?" Sage asked as she walked back over to the counter.

"Everything's fine," Ella said. "Let's

get back to it." She rubbed her hands together.

"You'll have to excuse us, Connor. I'm still training Ella, and there's lots more to go over," Sage said, gently pushing her brother toward the direction of the door.

He held up his hands. "I can take a hint. I'll see you ladies later."

Connor took one last look in Ella's direction. Although she appeared a bit steadier, there was still an unsettled expression on her face. She seemed wary, as if she was waiting for something bad to happen.

As he made his way back to the chocolate factory, Connor replayed the incident with Ella in his mind. Her reaction to Otis's vehicle backfiring had been over-the-top. He hadn't imagined her terrified response to the loud boom. It had been dramatic. What had she been so afraid of? So many possibilities flashed before him. None of the scenarios was pleasant. Maybe Ella had been hurt in the past by someone. And perhaps she'd come all the way to Owl Creek to get away from a turbulent situation with an ex. It chilled him to the bone to imagine Ella as the victim of domestic violence.

Warning bells were clanging in his head. He needed to avoid conflict-filled situations, especially since he was still grappling with the emotional fallout from his sister's recent return. He had no idea what Ella had been through, but he felt certain it had been intense. It radiated from her every time he was in her presence. Even though Ella Perez was the loveliest woman he'd ever laid eyes on, it was clear to him she'd come to town with burdens weighing her down. His family's painful history had taught him that he wasn't the sort of man who dealt well with secrets. Or lies.

There was something about Ella that

tugged at him, but he couldn't allow himself to get pulled into her world. Not now or ever.

Chapter Four

At the end of the day, Isabelle locked
up the front door of the chocolate shop.
Back in Miami she would have turned
on a security system, but as Sage had
explained to her, the chocolate shop
didn't have one. She turned the knob
just to make certain the establishment
was secured. It would be terrible if
someone broke in on her first day as
manager. Although Sage hadn't said it
in so many words, Isabelle had the feeling that Owl Creek didn't have a lot of
crime. It had been silly of her, then, to
get so frightened earlier at the sound of

the vehicle backfiring, but to her ears it had sounded like gunshots. Although Connor had been very comforting, she still felt terribly embarrassed. She worried that she'd made a misstep by overreacting.

It was hard to move forward, she realized, when she hadn't fully healed from the past. The shock of what she'd been through still affected her. Fear still cropped up at the most unexpected times. She knew it might be post-traumatic stress from having been victimized. Witnessing Saul's death and surviving the attempts on her own life had been devastating experiences. Isabelle prayed being in a safe haven like Owl Creek would help her heal. She didn't want to feel this way for the rest of her life.

Once she'd finished locking up, Isabelle took a quick look at her watch. It was just past five o'clock despite the darkened sky. She hadn't quite adjusted to the increased hours of darkness in Alaska. Her body was having a hard time acclimating to the lack of sunlight. Back in Florida it wouldn't get dark until after dinnertime.

Main Street was a charming area. It really did resemble something from a postcard. For such a small town there was an abundance of shops. There was a particular one that called out to her. Tea Time. From the moment she'd spotted the quaint tea shop, Isabelle had been intrigued by it. She'd always wanted to visit a tea emporium but had never had the opportunity back home. The townsfolk here led a quieter life.

She peered through the window, letting out a wistful sigh at the eye-catching decor. A soft light emanated from inside, providing a warm glow to the place. The place wasn't full of customers but there were a few people scattered around the dining room. In her direct line of sight were two women who were sitting at a table sipping tea and chatting. They seemed so happy simply spending time in each other's company. Suddenly, Isabelle's throat thickened as tears blurred her vision. Although she'd wanted to visit the tea shop, it hurt to realize she didn't have a single person with whom to share the experience. What she wouldn't give to sit down for tea with her sister or her best friend, Kara. She wondered if this ache would ever go away. Would she spend the rest of her life missing people and pretending to be somebody she wasn't?

Honestly, she wasn't sure what kind of existence that would be.

Isabelle turned away from the shop and made her way to the parking lot. It felt as if a huge weight was sitting on her chest. Her first day at the chocolate shop had been a success, but the very thought of going back to a quiet house made her want to sob. Although the marshals had done everything in their power to prepare her for a brand-new life in Alaska, she didn't feel very solid at the moment. She felt as if she was falling apart. Sitting by herself at a table at Tea Time would have only served to heighten her loneliness.

She started up the truck and began driving back to the house. Earlier she had overheard one of the customers saying that the roads were snow packed and a bit slippery due to the dipping temperature. She tried to cast off the feelings of doubt about driving on unfamiliar roads in less than desirable conditions.

Isabelle let out a groan as the GPS suddenly lost its connection. Talk about bad timing! She bit her lip as she reached a fork in the road. She was fairly certain she was supposed to bear to the right, but since she'd never traveled down this road in the dark it was a bit of guesswork.

As Isabelle made the turn, the truck's wheels skidded on the ice and she desperately tried to remember what to do in this particular situation. But before she could act, the vehicle swerved off the road, sideswiping a spruce tree and landing in a snowy ravine.

Isabelle sat still for a few moments, her hands tightly gripping the wheel. Her breathing was shallow. She'd been too frightened to let out a scream. And now she had no idea how to get help or even alert the local authorities as to her destination. Because of the darkened roads she was now thoroughly confused as to which road she was on.

She needed to call 911. Isabelle reached for her phone, frustration building inside her as she realized there was no cell signal. Isabelle let out a brittle-sounding laugh. Somehow she had managed to evade numerous attempts on her life by a hardened criminal, yet she was unable to find a way to help herself after a car wreck. She closed her eyes and began breathing deeply in and out.

Dear Lord. Please help me to not give in to this feeling of fear. I am stronger than I realize. With You by my side, I can do anything.

"Well, sitting here isn't going to solve this problem," Isabelle said, unfastening her seat belt as she prepared to exit the truck. Perhaps if she walked down the road a bit she might get a signal or come upon another driver or a nearby house. She looked down at her feet. She was thankful she'd switched from her work shoes to a pair of sturdy winter boots. Just as she reached for the door handle, bright headlights illuminated the truck. For a moment Isabelle waffled between gratitude and nervousness. Who had ridden up and stopped on the shoulder of the road? What if it was someone who meant to do her harm? Her heart began to beat at a rapid pace while her hands suddenly felt clammy.

Relax. She knew it was unlikely that Burke or his associates had located her in Owl Creek. That being said, it didn't stop her pulse from racing or the dark thoughts from materializing. Sweat broke out on her brow as she watched a tall figure exit the vehicle and slide down the incline toward her truck. With shaking fingers, she lowered the window just as the masculine voice washed over her. "Hey there. Are you all right? Are you hurt?"

Isabelle looked up and locked eyes with Connor. She let out a little sound of surprise at the sight of him. Gratitude rose up inside her at seeing a familiar face. Although she was thankful to be rescued, there was something about Connor North that made her feel as if he could see straight through all of her lies. And it made her incredibly nervous about being able to successfully reinvent herself in Owl Creek.

"Ella? What happened?" Connor asked as he peered into the truck window, needing to reassure himself that she wasn't injured. He'd spent a large portion of his day thinking about North Star Chocolate's newest employee, so it was a little jarring to come upon her on the side of the road with a smashed-up vehicle.

"I'm not hurt. The truck slid off the road. I didn't know what to do when I hit an icy patch. It felt like the truck had a mind of its own," she explained. Although she was trying to keep a stiff upper lip, Connor had the distinct impression she was unsettled. Her voice was trembling slightly and her big brown eyes were wide with alarm. A feeling of protectiveness swept over him. Crashing your truck on your first day of work in a new town had to be nerve-racking.

"Let's get you out of here," he said, extending his hand to pull her from her seat to a standing position. Isabelle reached for her oversize bag, murmuring a thank-you before slipping her hand into his. He walked her up toward level ground, holding on to her hand until she was standing by his vehicle. He only let go so he could hold open the passenger door for her. Once she was inside, Connor quickly made his way to the driver's side. He revved the engine, eager to make sure Ella was warm. She'd been shivering a few moments ago.

"I'll have the truck towed into town for repair," Connor said. "We're in a tricky area for cell service, so I might have to drive down the road in order to make the call."

"Oh, no. I need the truck to get to work."

"You live on Kodiak, right?" Connor

asked. He remembered his grandmother telling him she'd moved into the Barkers' former residence. He could easily picture her living in the charming home.

Ella nodded. "Yes, 10 Kodiak Lane. The sweet log cabin–style house with the bright blue chairs on the porch."

Connor smiled at her. "Good thing I live a few minutes away. We can figure something out. In the meantime, let me take you home. I'm sure you've had a long day."

She nodded. "It has been. I never imagined it would end with a car wreck." She made a face. "I've always been such a careful driver."

"Hang in there. Alaska roads can be tough to navigate."

"I'm not used to driving in snow."

Connor frowned. "I thought it snowed in parts of Arizona."

Silence stretched out between them before Ella answered. "Y-yes, it does, but not a lot," she explained in a shaky voice. She didn't sound very sure of herself, which once again raised a red flag with him. His friend Walt had lived in Flagstaff for two years and he'd told Connor they always experienced loads of snowy weather. Was it possible she really wasn't from that area? If that was the case, why would she fabricate something like that?

As his mind whirled with questions, he began driving in the direction of Ella's home. Connor knew these roads like the back of his hand. He'd been navigating them since he was seventeen years old. There wasn't anything quite like the freedom involved in getting behind the wheel and hitting the wide-open road.

"So, how was your first day at work?" Connor asked, trying to fill up the silence. A quick look in Ella's direction showed she was feeling more relaxed. Her lips were curved upward in a grin that made her even more attractive. If that was even possible.

"It was good. Really good, in fact. Sage and Beulah were amazing. Your sister walked me through everything and made me feel so comfortable."

Pride swelled inside him. Sage was such a giving person and a tremendous asset to the family business. "I imagine it's tough acclimating to a new town and a job all at once."

He heard a little sigh slip past her lips. "I'm not good with change. My life has been fairly predictable up till now," she admitted. "I'm not complaining, though. Owl Creek is a lovely place to start over."

Start over. There was something about her comment that made him curious. He wondered what exactly she'd left behind in Arizona and why she was eager to start over. The possibilities were endless. And even though he knew Ella wasn't obligated to disclose such personal information, a part of him still felt suspicious. What if she was running from something really awful that might compromise his family's business? He really needed to relax. He was becoming paranoid.

"My advice is to dive right in to the town. It has a lot to offer, from being a part of our choral group to dog mushing." He let out a throaty chuckle. "And if you're into bird watching, this town has some of the rarest species of birds in the country."

"Dog mushing? That sounds fascinating. I'm not sure I'm dog musher material, but I'd definitely love to watch sometime."

"That can be arranged. Owl Creek is hosting our fifth annual dog mushing race. It's a fun event. You shouldn't miss it."

"It sounds fun. Who can resist dogs?" Connor could hear the smile in her voice.

He turned to give her a quick look, needing to see her face lit up with joy.

Now at least he knew a little something about her. She was a dog lover. That was a start. He wasn't sure what it was about Ella that made him so curious about her backstory, but each and every time he was in her presence he found himself questioning if she was being truthful. The combination of his jaded nature plus Ella's evasiveness kicked his suspicions into high gear. Every time he felt tempted to scrutinize her résumé, he had to remind himself that she'd already been fully vetted before being offered the position.

In all likelihood he wasn't being fair to the beautiful newcomer, but some instinct warned him to keep a healthy distance. Easier said than done, he reminded himself. If she wasn't on the up-and-up, Connor needed to make sure his family wasn't exposed to anything that might hurt them. They'd already been through enough pain to last them several lifetimes. He wouldn't allow anyone to trick them again.

As he pulled up in front of Ella's home, he couldn't help but notice the huge spotlight lighting up the exterior of the house. It covered the entire perimeter of the front of the property. It struck him as the type of lighting someone might use to protect themselves against a home invasion. He stifled the urge to tell Ella that Owl Creek's crime rate was incredibly low. Breakins were unheard of. Perhaps in Arizona things were different. Or maybe she just needed reassurance as a single woman living on her own.

"Thanks for the lift," Ella said, jerking open the door and jumping down to the snow-covered ground.

He stepped out of the truck and walked around to the front of it, holding his phone up in the air. Connor frowned as he studied his cell phone. "I'm still not getting a signal."

Halfway down the walkway, Ella turned around and looked at him as if she was sizing him up. She raised her hand and motioned him over.

"No need to stand outside, Connor. Come on in and make the phone call from the house. You're doing me a favor after all by contacting the auto body shop."

"Thanks for the offer. I'll probably get a better signal from inside," he said.

By the time he caught up with her, she'd unlocked the door and stepped across the threshold. Connor walked in the house behind Ella, still feeling a bit surprised at her invitation. So far she had been very reserved, although she'd lightened up a bit during the ride to her house. Perhaps he should cut her a break. There wasn't anything wrong with being a private person, especially when she was a newcomer to town.

After all, it wasn't as if he'd told her his own life story. It wasn't fair to hold her to a higher standard.

Ella took off her boots and placed them on a nearby mat. Connor followed suit, not wanting to track snow on her gleaming hardwood floors.

The place was roomier than he remembered. The large living room had a comfy gray sofa with a matching love seat and a brightly colored rug on the floor. A few pieces of artwork were scattered on the walls. He didn't recognize any of the artists, but they were all vibrant works with splashes of color. The scent of pine cones lingered in the air. Although the place wasn't fully decorated, Ella had done a fine job of making it look homey and comfortable. It suited her.

Having been at the house before, Connor knew there was a stunning view of the mountains from the back deck. He enjoyed a similar view from his own place. Each and every morning he looked at the majestic peaks and thanked God for creating all of His beautiful masterpieces. Perhaps Ella would also find comfort in the breathtaking Alaskan vista. Although he was biased, Owl Creek was a magnificent place to call home.

Within minutes he'd made the call to Rusty's Auto Body Shop and made arrangements for Ella's car to be towed into town this evening.

Once he ended the call, he turned around to face her. "Rusty is going to take care of your truck for you. He's a really dependable mechanic. He's going to reach out to you once he takes a look at the damage."

"That's great. I appreciate it, Connor." She bit her lip. "I just hope the damage isn't too extensive."

"I'm no expert, but I don't think it's a total loss. Rusty won't charge you an arm and a leg either. His prices are reasonable. He's as solid as they come."

He watched as relief washed over her. Connor felt badly about the accident placing any kind of economic strain on her. Maybe he could arrange something with Rusty so the bill would be reduced. He shook off the thought. It wasn't his place to ride to the rescue, even if there was something about this woman that made him feel things he wasn't used to feeling.

"Why don't I swing by in the morning at eight?" he suggested. "I can drop you off at the shop, then head over to the factory."

Ella crossed her hands. "I'm so grateful, Connor. I'd hate to mess things up my first week on the job."

"No need to worry about that. Judging by the way my grandmother was singing your praises earlier today, you don't have anything to worry about." Beulah had talked nonstop about Ella and how she'd hired the perfect person for the position. His grandmother was a tough customer, so praise from her was rare.

"Would you like a cup of tea or some water?" she asked.

He held up his hand. "No, thanks. I need to head home so I can feed my pup."

"You have a puppy?" she asked. A look of surprise was etched on her face.

"Well, he's not actually a puppy. Bear is three and he's a Siberian husky." He let out a throaty chuckle. "He really enjoys dinnertime."

"I'm sure he does. Those are fairly large dogs." Ella giggled. The tinkling sound of it surprised him. It was light and airy. Laughter looked good on her. Her eyes lit up and there were little crinkles around her mouth. He couldn't take his eyes off her.

"Well, good night. I'll see you bright and early," Connor said, beating a fast path to the door. He felt as if he needed to get some air so he could think straight. More and more, Ella was growing on him, and he didn't know what to do to stop it. He felt helpless. Attraction was humming and pulsing in the air around them. He wondered if she felt it, too.

Connor resisted the impulse to turn around to see her one last time as she stood in the doorway. Only when he heard the door shut was he able to let out a sigh of relief.

On the way home Connor couldn't stop his thoughts from veering toward Ella. There was a reason he didn't want to feel anything romantic for her. Something about her just wasn't sitting right with him. Although her house was decorated stylishly and it exuded a cozy vibe, there were no pictures of family or friends. Not a single one. Where were the family photos? Mom and dad?

A sibling or two? A group of friends? Connor couldn't figure it out. Surely Ella had people in her life she was close to. Loved ones. Moments she wanted to highlight in her new home. The absence of those personal touches confounded him. Something was missing.

Who was Ella Perez? Other than being a transplant in Owl Creek and a newly hired manager for North Star Chocolates, she was an empty slate. He knew the weight of the past hung around his neck, but he was convinced Ella was hiding something. The fact that she was easy on the eyes wasn't going to distract him from the warning signs he was observing.

One way or the other, Connor was going to keep a watchful eye on Ella. Perhaps he was imagining things, but if he wasn't, he needed to be on alert. In the past his family had been victimized by a kidnapper and preyed on by people who sought to exploit their pain for profit.

He wasn't going to allow anyone else to hurt his family ever again.

Chapter Five

Isabelle woke up bright and early, determined not to make Connor wait for her. He'd been picking her up every morning for the past three days and dropping her off at the chocolate shop.

It was very sweet of him to do her a favor and she didn't want to push it by not being ready on time. Normally, Isabelle wasn't a morning person, but waking up at this hour allowed her to glimpse a glorious Alaskan sunrise— vibrant shades of orange and yellow bursting into view over the horizon.

Connor was proving to be a very kind

person, even though she'd caught him staring at her on several occasions as if she was a puzzle he wanted to solve. She'd slipped up a few times in his presence regarding her backstory. She wasn't sure if he'd picked up on it, but most likely she was being paranoid. He seemed like a very direct person, who would ask her if he thought her résumé wasn't on the up-and-up. Sometimes it felt as if she was walking around with a huge neon sign around her neck that declared her status as a WITSEC participant. It was hard not to wonder if she'd messed up big-time and inadvertently blown her cover. Up until her relocation to Owl Creek, Isabelle had no secrets to speak of. Now she was hiding almost everything about herself.

It wasn't smart of her to be around someone like Connor. His easy manner and charm tempted her to put down her guard and let him into her world. There was something about him that drew her in. As a result, it was a struggle to maintain an emotional distance from him. But there weren't many other people she knew here in town. Even though it would be tricky, she needed to forge friendships. She had to make a life for herself in Owl Creek, and without connections, she would be miserable.

Isabelle felt a burst of hope rising up inside of her. Beulah had invited her for a tour of the chocolate factory this morning. Ever since she was a kid, *Willy Wonka & the Chocolate Factory* had been her favorite movie. The prospect of getting a behind-the-scenes view of the North Star Chocolate Company's factory was thrilling.

She took a long sip of her cappuccino and let out a sigh of appreciation. What she loved most about her new house was her ability to enjoy breakfast and a wonderful view of the mountains while sitting at her kitchen table. Despite the intense feelings of homesickness she was battling, her new life was beginning to take shape. Her job at the chocolate shop kept her busy and focused. She hoped she could establish some sort of social life. Those connections would be vital if she was going to make things work here in Owl Creek.

Just as she finished washing and drying her breakfast dishes, she heard the sound of tires crunching over snow. After shrugging into her parka and stepping into her boots, Isabelle sailed out the door with her purse slung over her shoulder. She didn't want to examine too closely why the sight of Connor standing by the passenger-side door made butterflies flutter in the pit of her stomach.

"Good morning," he said with a smile as he opened the door for her. He was dressed in a dark wool coat and charcoal-gray slacks. An oatmeal-colored sweater peeked out from under his jacket. He always looked nice, but for some reason he appeared more handsome than ever today.

"Morning," she answered, shivering at the frigid temperatures. Would she ever get used to the weather in Alaska? Was it possible that this quaint village would someday feel like home? It seemed a million miles away from reality.

Once Connor was in the driver's seat, Isabelle turned toward him, and said, "You don't have to open the door for me every morning. It's pretty cold outside."

Surprise flared in his eyes. "What's the problem? I'm not complaining."

Suddenly, she felt foolish. "I don't mean to sound ungrateful." She shrugged. "I suppose I'm just not used to gestures like that."

"I'm sorry about that, but my folks raised my younger brother, Braden, and me to be gentlemen." He smiled at her. "If you see me around town, you might even catch me walking little old ladies across the street."

Isabelle chuckled. Connor's comment managed to defuse any awkwardness she'd been experiencing. "Sounds like you might be wearing a cape under that coat," she teased.

He raised a finger to his lips. "Shh. That's a well-kept secret here in town."

They continued the ride in companionable silence, with Isabelle soaking in the wintry scenery. Snow-covered trees—spruce, pine and birch—dotted the landscape. Once she'd found out she would be relocating to Owl Creek, Isabelle had done a bit of research on Alaska. She was now able to recognize several types of trees. She was hoping to spot some rare species of birds she'd read about. It still felt surreal that she'd come all the way to the last frontier to evade a killer's wrath.

As they drove, Isabelle wanted to ask Connor a million questions about the chocolate factory, but she refrained. Some things were just better to experience yourself. When Connor pulled into the parking lot minutes later, Isabelle could barely contain her excitement. As soon as Connor put his truck into Park, she practically vaulted from the vehicle, making it unnecessary for him to hold the door open for her.

She stopped walking and simply gazed up at the building. The factory was a large brick edifice with steam rising from the top of a stack. There was a grand set of granite steps leading to the entrance. A gold-and-brown sign with swirly writing hung by the entrance, welcoming visitors to the North Star Chocolate Company.

"Are you coming?" Connor asked, turning around to address her.

"O-of course," she said, trailing after him. "I wouldn't miss this for the world. I've been waiting my whole life for a Willy Wonka moment." Once the words escaped her lips, she felt a little bit goofy for expressing those sentiments.

Perhaps she should just try to be composed. She was visiting the factory in a professional capacity after all.

Connor's laughter rang out in the silence. "It's pretty special, but don't expect chocolate fountains or edible wallpaper. And there aren't any gardens full of lollipops," he teased. His reaction put her at ease. Clearly, as the heir to the chocolate empire, he understood her giddy feelings. She probably wasn't the first person to be so enthusiastic about visiting.

He beat her to the top of the stairs, then held the door open with a flourish, bowing at the waist as he said, "After you." She had the feeling he was making a teasing reference to her earlier comment about not needing doors held open for her. It showed her he was willing to make fun of himself.

Once she stepped through the doors, Isabelle sucked in a steadying breath. The sights, sounds and smells all competed with each other for her attention. She wasn't even sure where to look first. She let out a sigh of contentment as Connor steered her down a hallway with windows that overlooked conveyor belts and vats of chocolate. Isabelle felt like a little kid as she pressed her face against the glass. All the employees were dressed in baby blue uniforms with matching gloves and hairnets.

"Wow!" she said as employees plucked confections off the line and placed them in boxes, while others carried the boxes to another area. It looked like a finely honed operation. "This is quite the setup. Everyone is working in unison without skipping a beat."

"It's pretty spectacular, isn't it?" Connor asked. "We have the best employees in the world, if I do say so myself." Even though she hadn't done anything so far to earn praise, Isabelle felt buoyed by his words. It was nice to know he valued the employees.

She simply nodded, feeling over-whelmed by everything around her. The aroma of chocolate permeated the air. Isabelle felt certain she'd never smelled anything so delectable in her entire life. She couldn't put her finger on the specific type of chocolate floating in the air but it was probably an assortment of flavors. The smell was making her mouth water.

"It smells like my mama's chocolate-and-almond cake. It's a family favorite." A groundswell of nostalgia caused the words to burst from her mouth. She'd planned to avoid any mention of her family, but it wasn't as easy as she had imagined. Baking this particular delicacy was a tradition in their family going back generations. It was a huge part of her history. She would give anything to be seated at her family's large dining room table digging into a slice of the sweet baked good.

Connor nodded his head approvingly.

"I've never had the pleasure, but I've heard of it. If you decide to make it, don't forget to bring me a slice."

Although a part of her enjoyed the lighthearted banter between them, Isabelle continually had to remind herself to maintain a distance from Connor. From the first day they'd met, Isabelle had felt an attraction between them. If things weren't so messed up in her world, she wouldn't hesitate to flirt with Connor, perhaps even go out on a date with him if he asked. But her conscience wouldn't allow her to develop anything more than a friendship with him. It would be wrong to lead him on when she couldn't tell him the truth about being in the Witness Protection Program.

Honestly, she might be getting way ahead of herself. For all she knew, Connor had a long-term girlfriend in town, although she'd seen no signs of it. She'd overheard her staff talking about Connor being a sought-after bachelor in Owl Creek. Perhaps she was misreading things between them. Maybe she was the only one who felt something simmering in the air between them.

"You can enjoy the full tour later on, but I think we should head to my grandmother's office. I know she's eager to see you," Connor said, leading her toward a bank of elevators. When they reached the second floor, he led her down a hall of executive offices. They passed by one with Connor's name engraved on a brass plaque, but Isabelle didn't get an opportunity to get much of a glimpse of the interior. All she spotted was a tall bubble gum machine situated next to a sleek-looking desk. Connor slowed down when they reached a grand office a few doors down from his own. Located at the end of the corridor, Beulah's office was bright and welcoming, much like the woman herself.

"Ella! It's great to see you here," Beulah said as she rose from her chair. She quickly made her way around her desk and reached for Isabelle's hands, joining them together with her own.

For a second Isabelle felt startled by the greeting. She hadn't yet gotten used to being called Ella. It was still a bit jarring. Seeing Beulah felt wonderful, though. The older woman had been so kind and supportive on her first day. With her oversize personality and stately air, she reminded Isabelle of her own mother. They both exuded an air of confidence mixed with benevolence.

"Thank you for the invitation, Beulah. From what I've seen so far, this place is amazing," Isabelle gushed.

Beulah beamed at her praise. "I won't disagree with you. Not even a little bit. One of my smartest decisions was marrying my husband, Jennings. Not only did I get a cherished life partner, but it brought the North Star Chocolate Company into my life. His family created it, but I couldn't love it any more if I was born into it."

Connor put his arm around his grandmother. "You were destined to be a part of it."

Beulah beamed up at Connor. The interaction between them was heartwarming. She could feel the love flowing in the air.

"I would like to show you something, my dear." She strode over to her desk and pointed at a framed picture hanging on the wall. "This photo was taken over one hundred years ago when the factory first opened."

Isabelle's eyes widened as she studied the black-and-white photograph. At the time the image was taken, the factory was a simple brick building no more than a few thousand square feet. "I can't believe it's the same place. What a difference a century makes," Ella said.

"It might surprise you, but I wasn't born yet," Beulah said with a wink.

Connor and Isabelle joined in on the laughter. It was impressive to see such a distinguished businesswoman have the ability to laugh at herself. Connor was blessed to have her as his grandmother. Isabelle felt a burst of gratitude that she'd secured a position at Beulah's company.

"I'd like to show you some behind-the-scenes areas of the factory. It's a rite of passage for new employees," Beulah said, gleefully rubbing her hands together. "I might even share some trade secrets."

Connor leaned in toward Isabelle, speaking in a loud whisper as he said, "But then she'd have to make you disappear."

Connor's close proximity caused her pulse to quicken. A rich, woodsy scent hovered around him. Although Isabelle had met men like Connor before, she'd never met anyone who appeared to be the whole package. His dark hair and blue eyes combined with chiseled features and a rugged build made him one of the most attractive men she'd ever seen. He was smart and confident, with a loving family by his side. And judging by the lack of a wedding ring and local chatter, he was still single.

Beulah swatted her grandson. "I'd do no such thing. Follow me, Ella. There's plenty of intriguing aspects of this operation."

Isabelle nodded and walked over to Beulah. The CEO was a font of information and she couldn't wait to hear more from the older woman about the craft of making chocolate. She would be the perfect tour guide.

"I'm going to head back to my office and make a few phone calls," Connor said, glancing at his watch. "I'll see both of you in a little bit."

Isabelle felt a stab of disappointment. She loved Connor's whimsical side and the factory seemed to bring it out in him. She couldn't deny that Connor was quickly becoming a distraction. He tempted her to think of quiet nights by the fire and snowy walks on the town green.

What was it about Connor that brought out this side of her? She'd already decided to steer clear of any romantic entanglements in Owl Creek, knowing it would only serve to complicate her life if she became involved with anyone. But time after time her thoughts kept veering toward Connor.

For the next hour, Beulah walked Isabelle around the factory. There was so much to see behind the scenes. Isabelle was fascinated by the process of making such delicious chocolate from a simple cocoa bean. After seeing her keen interest, Beulah invited her to put on a uniform and take a turn on the assembly line. She was intrigued by the entire operation and the history of North Star Chocolates. Beulah rattled off so many details as they continued the tour, providing her with so much information that Isabelle's head was spinning.

Along the way Isabelle was introduced to numerous employees, all of whom appeared to hold Beulah in high esteem. Even though she was the CEO, Beulah was down-to-earth and likable. She treated everyone in the factory as if they were as important to the company as she was.

At the end of the tour Isabelle was treated to a new product that was being rolled out in the factory. It was the most delicious white hot chocolate cocoa created by Connor and his siblings. Beulah even tucked a few packets in a little pouch for Isabelle to take along with her.

As Beulah accompanied Isabelle back to the corridor where they'd started, she stopped in front of the office that Isabelle now knew belonged to Connor.

"I'm going to leave you here with my grandson. I hope you enjoyed the tour."

"It was truly wonderful," Isabelle said. "Thanks for making time for my visit. It means the world to me."

Beulah reached out and squeezed her hand. "It's impressive that you came all the way from Flagstaff to work for our company. I have a really good feeling about you, Ella. And I don't say that often."

Isabelle's heart sank. Guilt pricked at her. Beulah believed in her. The CEO of the North Star Chocolate Company had no idea that she'd hired a person who didn't actually exist. Ella Perez was a creation of WITSEC. Beulah's kindness made her feel like a complete and utter fraud. All she could do was stuff down the feelings of worthlessness and plaster a placid smile on her face.

"I appreciate the vote of confidence," Isabelle murmured.

"Thanks for coming, my dear. Don't

be a stranger. I hope to see you at some of our town events, starting with this weekend's festivities," Beulah said as she strode down the corridor. Isabelle knew she was referring to the dog mushing event that Connor had briefly mentioned. Signs promoting the event had been plastered all over Main Street and the town green. She didn't plan to miss it. It would provide her with a bona fide Alaskan experience.

Isabelle called out a feeble goodbye. Guilt threatened to swallow her up. She wished there weren't so many things about herself that she was hiding. Spending time with Beulah would be so much more rewarding if she could truly be Isabelle Sanchez. Beulah North was such a genuine person. She liked to think they had that in common, but at the moment, Isabelle couldn't credit herself with that attribute.

"Are you all right?" Connor asked,

concern threaded in his voice as he came to his office door.

"I... I'm fine," she murmured. But she really wasn't. Isabelle didn't enjoy feeling as if she was earning praise under false pretenses. The North family had treated her warmly ever since she'd arrived in their small Alaskan town. Beulah felt like an old friend, and she didn't want to ever let her down.

"You look a little shaken up," he said as he ushered her inside. "Can I get you anything? Perhaps some ice water?"

"No, I'm okay. Just a little headache," she said, pressing her fingers against her temple. She swung her gaze around Connor's office. It was a bright and airy space with colorful decorative touches. The tall bubble gum machine told her a lot about the man. It was a fun and imaginative touch. Maybe he was a kid at heart.

Connor followed her gaze. "That's my own homage to Willie Wonka. As a kid I always wanted a machine like this one in my bedroom." He flashed her a smile. "Clearly, my parents knew that it wasn't a good idea back then. I would have eaten them nonstop."

Isabelle grinned at the idea of a pint-size Connor yearning for a bubble gum machine. She could easily imagine a mini version of him. "Well, you finally made it happen. Good for you."

"Hey! Before I forget, I need to take your picture. HR usually does it for new employees, but I'm filling in for them this week. Let me grab my camera," he said. Connor turned toward his desk and began rifling through one of his drawers. After a few moments of fumbling around he located it.

Her picture? Her heart began beating a wild rhythm in her chest as her mind buzzed with questions.

"Why do you need to take my picture?" she asked. Isabelle could hear the panic in her own voice.

"You need an employee ID with your picture on it," Connor explained. A frown marred his brow. "It's standard procedure for new employees. And we might use the same photo for our company newsletter down the road. We always like to give a nice introduction to our new employees."

Fear gripped her. All of a sudden it felt as if she couldn't breathe. She hadn't anticipated this happening and she had no idea how to shut it down. What if having her picture taken placed her in a compromising position? Connor's casual mention of a newsletter was alarming. There were always so many what-ifs running around in her brain. It was nearly impossible to turn off the worry. What if someone recognized her from the company's newsletter? Just the idea of having her photo in the company's database made her feel uneasy. How many times had Marshal Kramer reminded her to keep a low profile? Although the idea of Vincent Burke and his cohorts tracking her down in Owl Creek seemed far-fetched, it still didn't stop the panic from rising up inside her. With Burke's request for a new trial pending, there was even more reason for him to want her out of the way. She was still in real danger.

"No!" she said in a heated voice. "I'm sorry! I really don't want to have my picture taken."

The vehemence in Ella's tone floored Connor. At first, he thought she was joking, but one look at the way her mouth was set in a thin, hard line convinced him otherwise. She was bristling with emotion. It radiated off her in waves. Some instinct warned him to tread lightly.

"Is there some reason you don't want your picture taken?" he asked. He shouldn't assume, but most women who looked like Ella were photogenic. He didn't understand what the big deal was at all. Was he missing something?

She shook her head, and said, "I... I probably look a wreck. I don't feel camera ready." He watched as she smoothed her hair back. She had a light sheen of perspiration on her forehead.

"You look great, Ella. Trust me, you have absolutely nothing to worry about." He was trying to put her at ease, but her body language didn't relax. She still looked as if she wanted to be anywhere else but here. Although he felt bad for her discomfort, he still felt stumped as to why she was making a big deal out of it. In the scheme of things, it shouldn't matter at all. Unless there was some reason why it mattered more than she was saying.

He prodded her. "Can I get a little smile? You're going to need this ID for the foreseeable future. You don't want to be frowning in the photo."

The corners of her mouth lifted, but

the emotion didn't make it all the way to her eyes. It didn't feel genuine. He snapped a few photos, then lowered the camera and studied the images. Just as he'd suspected, the camera had captured Ella's beauty as well as her discomfort. "I'm sure one of these can work for your ID."

She knit her brows together. "That's good. So, you're just using the photo for my ID? Nothing else?"

"I promise you, we're not going to put it on the front page of the *Owl Creek Gazette*. And our newsletter is a mail out that is only sent out to people who work for us, so you're not going to become famous." His tone was teasing, but he wasn't sure the situation was funny. Ella was clearly ruffled. Why was she acting so camera shy? All morning he'd been able to put aside his niggling doubts about Ella. Until now. Suddenly his mind was drifting to all the strange things he'd observed about her ever since they'd met. He continued to have so many questions about her.

Ella's shoulders noticeably sagged with relief. "I should probably head back to the shop. Being here was a nice treat, but I don't want to overstay my visit."

"You're welcome here anytime," Connor said. And despite his doubts, he meant it. Ella was a breath of fresh air in Owl Creek and at the chocolate company. When a person grew up in a small Alaskan town they were part of a tight-knit community. Connor had always loved that aspect of his hometown. On the downside, you knew everyone, and in return, they knew everything about you. There weren't too many opportunities to peel back the layers. Maybe that was what was really bothering him about the beautiful newcomer. She seemed to have a wall up, despite the sweet air she exuded.

"Let me walk you back to the entrance," Connor said. "These hallways can be a bit tricky."

Ella nodded and walked alongside him. Along the way, employees gave them hearty greetings and a few times she threw out questions about the factory. She appeared to be genuinely interested in the workings of his family's company.

Connor couldn't help but notice the curious looks in Ella's direction. As a newbie to the small town, Ella stood out from everyone else who'd been born and bred in Owl Creek. Folks were bound to be curious about her. He wasn't sure what exact feelings he was battling against when a few male employees smiled extra long in her direction. Was he being overly protective or slightly annoyed at their interest in her?

"Thanks for everything. I talked to Rusty and it's going to be a little bit longer to make the repairs." Ella winced. "It seems I really did some damage in the accident. He had to order some special parts from Anchorage."

"It's not a problem. We're neighbors. I'm available for as long as you need me." Ella seemed beholden to him for the daily rides to town and back, but in reality she was doing him a favor. She was keeping him company and brightening up his day. He enjoyed hearing about her daily adventures at the chocolate shop and finding out about the new trends in customer purchases. It felt as if he was seeing things through a brand-new pair of eyes. He planned to be a creative force at North Star Chocolates for the remainder of his working life. One day he would take over the reins from Beulah, since his parents had already decided they didn't wish to be at the helm. He planned to inject his own special brand of creativity and passion into the company. Until that time he was going to be a sponge and soak up all he could regarding the business.

"As long as it's not an imposition. As soon as I get the truck back I plan to practice driving on the roads near my house just to get some experience." Ella's expression was sheepish. He sensed she was still beating herself up about the accident.

"Don't stress yourself about it. You'll get the hang of these Alaska roads in no time."

"I sure hope so," she said with a shake of her head. "I'm eager to explore Owl Creek during my off time. I've heard about the wonderful birds that inhabit this town and I'd love to see some of them."

"This place has a lot to offer. It's not flashy or grand in any way, but it has a lot of charm. Before you know it, Owl Creek will feel like home."

A look of sadness crept over her face. As quickly as he'd noticed her expression it was gone, replaced by a serene look. "Thanks for the pep talk. See you later," she said as she headed outside into the blustery morning.

He stood inside and watched as Ella walked down the steps and headed in the direction of Main Street. Even though he had back-to-back meetings scheduled and countless emails to catch up on, he felt an urge to push past the doors and take a walk with Ella to the chocolate shop. Along the way he could point out interesting landmarks, specialty shops and tell her a little bit about the town's history. Maybe he could get her to laugh by telling her about the prank he, Hank and Gabriel had played on the townsfolk one Christmas. It had involved a Nativity scene, six roosters and a Cabbage Patch doll. Even though they'd gotten in trouble for it, the Three Amigos still chuckled about it to this day.

There was something about Ella that made him feel the need to be carefree and seize the moment. She had the type of beauty that wasn't just on the surface. It seemed to come from deep inside of her. His grandmother certainly seemed drawn to her, judging by the expression stamped on Beulah's face. That had to mean something about Ella's character, he told himself. His grandmother didn't suffer fools gladly, and she had a knack for sniffing out insincerity. So was Ella the real deal after all?

Connor shook off the notion of leaving the factory and catching up to Ella. Regardless of how she made him feel, he knew there was way more to her than met the eye. Every instinct was warning him to tread lightly. He wasn't a man who took chances. And something told him that Ella Perez was a risk he couldn't afford to take.

Chapter Six

Once Isabelle made it back to Main Street, she found herself slowing down as she passed by Tea Time. The elegant shop beckoned her to go in and treat herself to oolong tea and a plate of cucumber sandwiches and scones. It would be such an amazing indulgence. If she hadn't already spent hours at the factory, she would have gone inside and basked in the lovely surroundings of the tea emporium. As it was, she really needed to scoot.

"If you're wondering if you should go in, I would highly encourage it."

Isabelle spun around at the sound of the familiar voice. Sage was standing behind her with a wide grin etched on her face. She radiated a pure joy that caused Isabelle to yearn to find such serenity in her own life. What would it feel like, she wondered, to experience life in this amazing town with nothing to hide? She envied Sage's seemingly blissful life while at the same time acknowledging it couldn't have been granted to a kinder person.

"Hi, Sage. You caught me in the act. It isn't the first time I've looked longingly through this particular window," she admitted with a chuckle. "This place looks so appealing, although I've never had a chance to go in."

"Well, now you do. Come on inside with me. I have business with the owner, Iris Lawson. I'd love for you to meet her."

Sage bit her lip. "I really should head back to the chocolate shop. I've been at the factory all morning." She took a quick look at her watch. "This morning has just flown by."

"Just for a few minutes. I promise," Sage said, taking her by the hand and leading her through the doorway. Isabelle didn't put up much of a fight. Her curiosity to see the interior of Tea Time had been pricking at her for days now. She would check out the establishment, but she wouldn't linger for long.

As she trailed after Sage, Isabelle soaked in all the details of the tea emporium. The first thing that drew her attention was the vintage chandelier shimmering from the ceiling. Intimate tables were adorned with beautiful tablecloths and lace doilies. Flowers sat in a small bouquet on each table. Beautiful gold curtains and lush velvet chairs added an air of refinement. Peering in from the front window didn't do this place justice.

"Isn't it magnificent?" Sage asked.

Isabelle nodded. A sweet smell hovered in the air. She inhaled deeply as she tried to pin down the scent. It wasn't a single aroma, she realized. It was a myriad of tea scents all floating in the air. This, she thought, was paradise. If only she had time to partake in the experience.

"It feels like we've stepped into another era. Those drapes remind me of something from the Jazz Age," Isabelle remarked. She loved reading historical novels set in the 1920s. Tea Time would fit right into the setting of one of her favorite books.

Suddenly, a tall woman with brown skin began making a beeline in their direction. With her animated features and an almost regal bearing, she exuded pure elegance. "Sage. It's great to see you. I've been wondering when you would stop by."

"Hey, Iris. I'm sorry it took me so long to circle back. Things have been crazy lately. I wanted to check in with you regarding the wedding shower Rachel and I are throwing for Piper."

Iris clapped her hands together. "Rachel has been finalizing some of the details, so I think we're really in good shape." Iris turned toward Isabelle, shooting her a curious look.

"Oops. Where are my manners? Iris, I'd like to introduce you to Ella Perez. She just relocated here from Arizona." Sage grinned. "She's working at the chocolate shop. Ella, this is Iris Lawson, the owner and creative genius behind Tea Time."

Iris beamed at the compliment. "Ella, it's such a pleasure to meet you. It's wonderful to see a young person like yourself planting roots here."

"Your place is lovely, Iris. Every time I walk by it just pulls me in," Isabelle said. "Your interior decorating aesthetic is fantastic."

Iris beamed. "Thank you. In my youth

I wanted to go to design school, which wasn't possible, so I was able to fulfill all of my decorating dreams right here at my shop."

"Iris's son, Gabriel, is one of my husband Hank's closest friends," Sage explained. "And he recently got married to Rachel, who is a dear friend and an amazingly skilled nurse. She's helping me plan Piper's bash."

"And along with Rachel came two beautiful little girls, Faith and Lizzie. We're all so blessed," Iris said. "Our family has blossomed in the last few months."

"It sounds like it," Isabelle said. Family was everything. Watching it grow and expand through marriage and children had always been so gratifying for Isabelle's own mother. She felt a pang at the thought of missing out on motherhood.

"Well, why don't the two of you take a

seat?" Iris asked. "I just made the most enticing batch of lemon bars."

Isabelle wished she could take Iris up on her offer. "Any other time I would love to, but I really have to get back to work. I've been away all morning."

"That's a shame." She wagged her finger at Isabelle. "I'm going to give you a rain check. Come back anytime and there'll be a table waiting for you. In the meantime, I'm going to wrap up some lemon bars for you to take with you. On the house. It's my welcome to Owl Creek gift."

As Iris quickly made her way back to the kitchen, Isabelle turned toward Sage. "The owner is just as lovely as the establishment."

"She must like you," Sage said. "Iris has a bit of a sharp edge at times. She's a little like my grandmother in that regard," she confessed.

"Something tells me they're both strong women." Isabelle wished she could be a little bit more like the two older women. These days she always felt as if she was coming apart at the seams. She needed to dig down deep and draw strength from God. Ever since this ordeal began, He had been with her. Back when she was working at the club in Miami, Isabelle hadn't lived a faith-filled existence. That had all changed after witnessing a murder.

Lord, please grant me strength. I have miles to go on this journey. If I'm going to stay in Owl Creek, I need fortitude. I need to be as strong as an oak tree.

"Hey!" Sage said in a raised voice that drew Isabelle out of her thoughts. "I just had a great idea. Why don't you come to Piper's bridal shower?"

"I know who Piper is. She's a sweetheart. I met her at the Snowy Owl. She's the owner, right?"

"Yes. That place is her pride and joy. Piper is my husband Hank's sister. She's marrying my brother, Braden."

Isabelle shook her head, feeling confused. "So, wait. Does that mean she'll be your sister-in-law twice over?"

Sage chuckled. "Yes, it does. It's a little confusing, but I couldn't ask for a better friend than Piper. She already feels like my sister."

Isabelle experienced a twisting sensation in the region of her heart. She knew all too well about the powerful bonds of sisterhood. Not being able to talk to her own sister made her feel as if she was missing her right arm. She fought past the lump in her throat. "That's wonderful. A sister is a lifelong treasure."

"I agree," Sage said with a smile. "She would be thrilled to have you there. Please join us."

"Oh, no," she exclaimed. "I wouldn't want to intrude on such an intimate gathering of friends and family."

"You'll be an invited guest, Ella. In Owl Creek we don't stand on ceremony." She crossed her hands in prayer-like fashion. "Please come. It will give you an opportunity to meet some very special people. I know firsthand what it feels like to be a stranger in a new town. It's not easy."

Isabelle heard the sincerity in Sage's voice. It sounded like she had been in Isabelle's shoes at one point in her life. That knowledge made her feel even closer to Sage, even though they had only recently met. And although she didn't want to admit it to herself, she yearned to find friends in Owl Creek. The idea of attending a party at the tea shop and meeting the residents in a festive setting was extremely appealing to her.

Just then Iris returned with a little white box tied up with black ribbons. "Here are the lemon bars. Enjoy them," she said, handing them over to Isabelle.

"Thank you, Iris," Isabelle said. "What a thoughtful gesture." With every kind act performed by one of the residents of Owl Creek, her heart began to open up a little more to the idea of becoming a member of this community. Their generosity filled up her soul.

"I hope to see you at the town festivities this weekend. Dog mushing. Crepes. Ice cream. Arts and crafts." She clapped her hands together. "You'll have a ball!" With a smile, Iris turned back toward the dining room and began stopping at tables and checking in on her customers.

Isabelle looked over at Sage. "If you're sure it's okay, I'd love to come to the party," Isabelle said. Joy fluttered in her chest. It was so nice to feel included. She couldn't remember the last time she'd attended a social event. Her entire life had collapsed in an instant back in Miami, and her world had gotten very small.

"Great!" Sage said, clapping her hands together. "The party is a week from this Saturday at noon. Don't worry about bringing a present. Only your presence is required. And don't forget it's a surprise."

"Perfect. I really need to get to the shop before the staff thinks I've gone missing." With a wave of her hand, Isabelle strode toward the exit. As she made her way down the street, Isabelle's heart felt lighter than it had been in months. So far, today was shaping up to be a banner day. Even though her transition from her old life in Miami felt a bit shaky at times, she had to concede that certain things were moving her in a good direction. Perhaps happiness was in her future. If she could just manage to keep looking forward and not dwell on the past, maybe it would be within reach.

When the sign for the chocolate shop came into view, Isabelle's thoughts turned to Connor. It was becoming increasingly difficult not to think about him. Seeing him every day surely wasn't helping matters. She let out a groan of frustration. If she had a checklist for a love interest, Connor would score a perfect ten. But she couldn't imagine delving into a relationship with him, all while hiding her truths under the surface. The North family had been so good to her by employing her and encouraging her to become an integral part of Owl Creek. Pretending to be someone she wasn't still felt wrong on so many levels, even though it had been borne out of necessity.

Even though she was safe in her new Alaskan life, Isabelle still had vivid nightmares about Saul's death and the attempts on her life. In some of the dreams Isabelle hadn't managed to flee the nightclub. Instead, she'd met the same end as Saul at the hands of Burke. She still felt broken about all she'd gone through. It was hard not to question whether she had done the right thing by testifying and agreeing to participate in the Witness Protection Program. It had turned her entire life upside down, as well as the lives of those near and dear to her. It still felt surreal to her to be living as Ella Perez.

She was still grieving the loss of Isabelle Sanchez. There was no way of knowing if she would ever get used to being this new version of herself.

Connor bit into his crab cakes and let out a groan. As usual, the menu at the Snowy Owl did not disappoint. Although he was no slouch in the kitchen, Connor couldn't compete with the diner's offerings.

Piper stood by the table, grinning at his reaction. "They're good, huh?"

"If my brother wasn't already marrying you, I might just propose so you could make me these for the rest of my life," Connor said.

"That's about as likely as a heat wave in December." Braden North stepped up and wrapped his arms around Piper's waist, then leaned down to place a kiss on her cheek. "She's taken."

"I am indeed," Piper said, grinning at her fiancé.

"Settle down, little brother." Connor made a face at Braden. "I'm trying to eat my dinner. Take that kissy-face stuff to another booth."

Piper rolled her eyes. "Let me know if you guys need anything else." She walked off toward the kitchen with Braden by her side. Connor's gaze trailed after them. He still couldn't believe the lifelong best friends had fallen in love. Connor hadn't seen it coming at all, but he knew they were as perfect for one another as a couple could be. Contentment shimmered off them in waves.

What would it feel like to know his destiny was tied up in another human being? He imagined it would be epic. When he looked at Braden, it seemed as if his brother's heart had grown by leaps and bounds. Loving Piper had brought out the very best in him. Hank had said the same about his sister.

Knowing he needed to focus on why he'd met up with his best friends for dinner, Connor turned back to Hank and Gabriel sitting across from him at the table. "Okay, now that they're gone we can keep planning the bachelor party."

"I'm not sure about your idea. It doesn't sound fun to me. Maybe we can stage an elaborate game night," Hank suggested.

Connor groaned. "Come on, guys. Have a little creativity. This is supposed to be my little brother's prewedding send-off. Who wants to sit around playing checkers?"

Gabe let out a snort. "No one said anything about checkers. We just don't think Piper would appreciate placing her husband-to-be in any jeopardy."

Connor scoffed. "Braden has done

every extreme sport you can imagine. I don't think that a little night skiing would be a problem."

Hank shook his head. "Connor, you need to start brainstorming again. Considering how Jack died, I think it could come across as insensitive."

Connor let out a groan and slapped his forehead. "I have no idea where my head is at. That would really be problematic. Not to mention downright inconsiderate. Maybe we can do a bowling night and rent out the place just for the party. With food and music, it could be just right. Thanks for the save, guys."

Piper's father and Hank's stepfather, Jack Miller, had passed away after a snowmobile accident on one of the mountain trails. It had caused a huge rift between Piper and Braden when it was revealed that Braden had been arguing with her father shortly before the tragic accident. Thankfully, they had sorted things out and reconciled. Their spring wedding was mere weeks away.

"No problem. We're all excited that Braden and Piper are making it official." Gabriel grinned as he put a forkful of rosemary potatoes in his mouth.

Hank frowned. "He better treat my little sister right or he's going to answer to me." The menacing expression stamped on his face gave way to a smirk when he couldn't keep a straight face. Gabe and Connor began chuckling along with him.

"I've always wanted to say that. You know I think the world of Braden," Hank admitted.

Connor grinned. "The feeling is mutual. He's looked up to the three of us ever since he was in diapers," Connor said, struggling to keep his emotions in check. Growing up in the shadow of a tragic event such as his sister's kidnapping had forged a strong bond between the two brothers. Although they were now traveling on different paths since Braden was opening a business specializing in Alaskan adventures, the love between them couldn't be any stronger. Watching him fall head over heels in love with his best friend had been awe-inspiring. The happy couple was also working together with Piper's pie business, Pie in the Sky.

"So, how are things going with the new girl in town? Ellen? I heard she's working at the chocolate shop," Gabe said.

"Ella," he said, quickly correcting his friend. "She seems to be acclimating well to our little town. She had an accident with her truck so I've been giving her a lift to work until Rusty makes the repairs," Connor explained.

"That's too bad she had a wreck," Gabe said. "I hope she's all right."

"She didn't have so much as a scratch, but the truck wasn't as fortunate," Connor answered. "I'm just praying she doesn't get jittery about driving on these icy roads. I remember when I had that accident back in high school. It took me a long time to work up the courage to get back behind the wheel."

Hank nodded. "Sage is raving about her and how well she's doing at the chocolate shop. I think my wife has found a new friend."

"That's great. Sage is the perfect person for Ella to bond with." Just the thought of the two women becoming friends made him smile. His sister was compassionate and understanding. "It must be challenging being new to Owl Creek. Most of the townsfolk have been in each other's pockets for all of our lives."

Hank took a big swig of his hot chai. "Something tells me you're doing some bonding of your own with Ella, judging by that look on your face."

"We're just friends," Connor said, not wanting Hank or Gabe to get the wrong idea. He knew all too well how fast rumors spread here in town. "Even a blind man can see she's beautiful," he conceded, "so there's a definite attraction. I feel this pull in her direction that makes me want to be around her."

Gabe leaned forward across the table. "I can hear a 'but' coming."

Connor let out a sigh. "At the risk of being considered paranoid, I'm pretty certain she's running from something in her past." He looked back and forth between his friends, waiting for skeptical expressions to appear on their faces. When it didn't happen, he continued to speak. "I can't say for certain what it is, but something doesn't feel right about her backstory."

"Maybe she had a bad breakup," Gabe said. "People relocate all the time due to their personal lives."

"True." Connor sighed. "Trouble is, the only woman who makes me feel anything romantic at all these days is Ella."

"And why is that a problem?" Hank asked.

"Because all of my instincts are telling me she's sitting on a mountain of secrets. I can't put my finger on it, but our new employee isn't as she appears to be. And it's putting up a wall between us."

"What do you think she's hiding?" Gabriel prodded.

Connor shrugged. "I have no idea. Something just doesn't feel right. Her reason for coming all this way to Alaska is a bit shaky."

Hank scratched his jaw. "People move all the time. Maybe her old life wasn't working, and she wanted a fresh start. It's not far-fetched at all. We have several residents who transplanted here from other places."

Connor let out a frustrated sound. "Okay. It's possible I'm just putting up roadblocks, but my instincts are telling me something is off with her. And I have to admit, it has crossed my mind that she could be involved in something illegal."

"As a member of law enforcement, I have to caution you against going down that trail without evidence. It's a huge leap," Hank said.

"What your family has been through would make anyone a bit jaded," Gabe added. "I know when Sage revealed herself as your long-lost sister, you were the last family member to believe it was true. You're a pragmatic person, Connor, but sometimes you tend to see cracks when there really aren't any. Just keep that in mind."

"He's right," Hank chimed in. "And the problem is, you could be blocking your greatest blessing in the process."

His greatest blessing. Lately, Connor had been thinking about his future and dreaming of a life different from the one he was leading. He loved his job, adored his family and his hometown, yet there was a void in his life that nothing had been able to fill. Although he would never admit it to his best friends, he was lonely. He'd never yearned for love before, but he knew it was the missing ingredient in an otherwise charmed life. Keeping women at a distance was his strong suit, but it hadn't helped him move forward on his journey.

Could Ella become someone special in his life? Perhaps he was foolish to even think it, since they barely knew one another. Another part of him couldn't help but wonder. He felt a strong, inexplicable pull in her direction. If he gave it a chance, would something develop between them? He had no idea. Keeping her at arm's length seemed practical to him, but he couldn't discount Gabriel's and Hank's comments. If he continued to do as he'd always done, the path he was taking would lead him to a lifetime of loneliness.

Chapter Seven

It was a beautiful January evening in Alaska and Chinook Woods was one of the loveliest places she'd ever seen. Isabelle had decided to attend the dog mushing event that featured a well-known dog musher, Ace Reynolds, who had ties to Owl Creek. Despite the frigid temperature, no snow was falling from the pewter-colored sky. Although Isabelle thought the fluffy white stuff was pretty, she still hadn't gotten used to being surrounded by it. She inhaled the pristine air, then exhaled. It was true, she realized, what folks said about the

Last Frontier. The air felt purer than any other place she'd ever been.

Day by day she was learning how to dress for the Alaskan climate. Tonight she had taken great care with her attire. She had decided on a black turtleneck sweater, a pair of black thermal leggings and a cranberry-colored parka. A pair of genuine Alaskan Lovely boots completed the outfit. The boots had been delivered to her house courtesy of Beulah. The gesture had been so thoughtful and kind. She felt very grateful that she'd landed in a town filled with sweet-natured people who never stopped going out of their way for her. Just this morning Rusty the mechanic had reached out to her, telling her that his repairs on her truck would be completed by tomorrow. He'd even offered to take her out on the icy roads for a few driving lessons. It had been such a heartwarming gesture, especially when Rusty told her he'd taught all of his four daughters how to drive on snow-slick-ened Alaskan roads.

Each act of kindness made her feel one step closer to becoming part of the Owl Creek community. It would make all the difference in the world to her if she was embraced by the residents. And she would try her best to recipro-cate, even though she was having a bit of trouble opening up. She was so afraid of making another misstep and arous-ing suspicion.

Isabelle had graciously accepted a ride to town from one of her staff members, Lissa Montgomery. She hadn't bothered to ask Connor, since she already felt so indebted to him for all of his transporta-tion assistance. She didn't want to make him feel as if he was her permanent chauffeur. And what if he'd brought a date tonight? She would have felt like an awkward third wheel. The idea of it made her shudder.

She could see him across the way,

talking with two men she recognized from her first visit to the Snowy Owl Diner. The three men were all extremely animated. If she had to guess, Isabelle would say they were close friends of his. They seemed so comfortable in each other's presence. That's what she hoped to find here in town. A friend she could laugh with and share special moments with.

"Ella! I'm so thrilled you could make it!" Sage, accompanied by Piper and a striking woman with warm brown skin and a lovely smile, strode over to her. Sage leaned in to envelop her in a tight hug.

Isabelle grinned. "I'm happy to be here. I was just contemplating whether to grab some hot apple cider or a hot cocoa."

"I'd go for the hot cocoa," Piper said. "It's straight from the chocolate factory."

"And indescribably yummy," the other woman added.

Sage introduced the woman. "This is Rachel Lawson. Rachel, this is Ella Perez."

"Nice to meet you," Rachel said, extending her mittened hand.

"You as well," Isabelle said, recognizing the woman's name as that of Iris's daughter-in-law.

"Why don't we get some of the hot chocolate?" Piper suggested. "I've been on my feet all day at the diner. I need a little pick-me-up."

Rachel looped her arm through Piper's in a show of support. "Aww. You deserve it."

As they walked toward the concession stand, Isabelle fielded questions about how she was acclimating to life in Owl Creek.

"Every day gets a little easier. The weather and the lack of sunlight are the two hardest challenges. I love working at the chocolate shop. And I'm not just saying that because your family owns it, Sage," she teased, drawing laughter from the three women.

Sage nodded. "I'm glad you're settling in so nicely."

"Everyone has been very welcoming," Isabelle answered. It still astounded her how the townsfolk were being so warm and helpful.

"Are you single?" Rachel asked. Although the question was a bit abrupt, Rachel exuded an air of kindness that made the inquiry palatable.

"Very much so," Isabelle said. "I haven't had a boyfriend in years," she admitted. For so long Isabelle had thrown herself into her work at the club, never stopping to acknowledge how her hectic work schedule and unorthodox hours had made a relationship impossible.

"Something tells me you might not

be single for long," Rachel said with a knowing look etched on her face.

Isabelle quickly spoke up. The last thing she needed or wanted was prodding about her romantic life. "I'm not really looking for a relationship."

Piper let out a loud chuckle. "That's what I said right before I fell in love with my best friend. Now we're getting married in a few weeks."

"Life and love has a way of changing all of our plans," Sage said. "None of us were looking for love, but it sure found us."

Piper and Rachel both nodded their heads in agreement.

"We could put our heads together and make you a match!" Rachel said in a voice brimming with exuberance.

"That would be so much fun!" Piper said with a squeal.

"And since we know everyone in town, we could really home in on the best prospects," Sage added. Excitement hung in the air as the women hatched a plan for Isabelle's love life.

Isabelle shook her head. "I hate to rain on your parade, but I can't think of anything that I'd dislike more than a fix-up. I've been on some blind dates that were the stuff of nightmares. I promised myself I'd never go down that road again."

Isabelle didn't miss the look of disappointment stamped on all three faces. They sounded so well-meaning. She knew they were trying to do something nice for her. Shame threatened to swallow her up. But none of them had any idea that she wasn't like them. Her whole foundation in Owl Creek had been built on lies. Who would want to be in a relationship with a woman who couldn't even tell the truth about her own name?

"I'm sorry," she apologized. "Right now, I just want to focus on my job and getting acclimated to Alaskan living."

"Don't fret on our account," Rachel

said. "You're a beautiful woman, Ella. You radiate pure positivity." She winked at her. "You'll be just fine."

As they stood in line and ordered their cocoa, Isabelle thought about what her new friends had suggested. Though a part of her would love to be coupled up, it just wouldn't be fair for her to become involved with someone when she couldn't be honest with him about being in the Witness Protection Program. It was hard to imagine living happily-ever-after without complete truth and transparency.

And ye shall know the truth, and the truth shall make you free. It was one of Isabelle's favorite Bible passages. Lately, she had been reciting it several times a week and drawing strength from it. She still harbored a little kernel of hope that her situation might change one day. Every night she prayed to get her life back.

Isabelle let out a ragged sigh. Her life

here in town would be so different if she wasn't in Alaska under the guise of being a completely different person. What would it be like, she wondered, to be as carefree as Sage, Rachel and Piper? They all seemed to lead such happy and contented lives, free of problems or worries. A feeling of envy rose up inside her. She missed the days when her biggest concern was whether she was going to get a raise at work. It was hard not to wish for simpler days when she didn't have to struggle to keep her story straight or look over her shoulder in fear.

And it was even more difficult to imagine being drawn toward someone in Owl Creek other than Connor. Even though she knew better than to try to pursue anything romantic with him, she couldn't deny his massive appeal or her own excitement whenever they were together. She wasn't sure there was a man in Owl Creek who could compare to him.

* * *

Connor stood back and surveyed all of the revelry taking place in front of him. He was grinning so widely the sides of his mouth were beginning to feel the strain. There were so many people who'd come out tonight to support the dog mushing event. It's what he loved most about Owl Creek. The townsfolk truly loved gatherings where they could socialize and support one another. All the proceeds from this evening were going to support rescue dogs through the outreach of Best Friends, a local veterinary clinic in town owned by Maya Roberts.

Maya had recently returned to Owl Creek in order to take over the practice from her dad, Vance Roberts, who had made the decision to retire. So far, she was impressing everyone in town with her skill and generous heart. Her advocacy on behalf of rescue dogs had almost convinced him to adopt a four-legged companion. He wasn't sure Bear was ready for another dog in the house, but Connor still had his eye on adopting. Once his Siberian husky was better trained, Connor was going to reach out to Maya.

Try as he might, Connor couldn't manage to look away for long from Ella, who was standing with Sage, Rachel and Piper. His gaze kept veering back to her. Seeing the foursome amiably chatting made him happy. Ella needed connections in town in order to properly settle in to her new life. She couldn't befriend three more fabulous women than the ones she was with at the moment.

"So, why are you standing over here when Ella is over there? Clearly she's on your mind judging by the way you keep staring at her." Gabe jutted his chin in Ella's direction. Connor swung his gaze her way for what felt like the hundredth time. In her cranberry-colored parka, matching hat, boots and black leggings, she looked ready for the Alaskan elements. Fashionable and functional. Always stunning.

"I'm not staring. Can't a person just look around at the scenery?" Connor asked through gritted teeth.

"Did you bring her here tonight? I thought maybe she was your date," Braden inquired in a loud voice.

Connor glared at his brother. "We are not on a date. Can you keep your voice down? The last thing I need is to have everyone in town spreading that rumor around. You know how it goes."

Hank, Braden and Gabriel had identical grins on their faces. He could tell they didn't believe a word he was saying about not being paired up with Ella.

"Come on! It's not funny. We're not an item!" Connor protested.

"Not yet," Hank said. "But with your smooth moves, it's only a matter of time." He wiggled his eyebrows, garnering more laughter from the group.

"You guys don't know what you're talking about," he snapped. There were way too many reasons why a relationship between them was an impossibility. Above all else, he didn't trust her. There were too many red flags popping up. Her nervousness about having her ID picture taken had been bizarre.

"It's obvious you like her. You've had the same tell since we were in elementary school," Gabe said with a smirk.

Connor frowned at him. "What are you talking about?"

Braden pointed at his feet. "The way you rock back and forth on your heels. It's a dead giveaway that you're into Ella. You've been doing it ever since she got here."

Gabe and Hank nodded in agreement.

Gabe placed his hand on Connor's shoulder. "I hate to break it to you, but two of the Three Amigos have settled down. And Braden will be married in no time at all. You might be next. You've got to be open to it, though," Gabe said. "Don't stick your head in the sand."

Connor let out a groan. It wasn't as if he hadn't already thought about the fact that Gabriel, Hank and Braden had all found the loves of their lives, while he'd been sitting on the sidelines. How could he forget when his mother kept hinting about his single status? It was beginning to grate on him. "I'm not in any rush to settle down. That's not my goal." He'd been using this stock excuse for years, but for some reason it no longer felt one hundred percent true. Seeing everyone else in his inner circle pair off had caused a shift inside him. He no longer wanted to walk through life alone.

"And that's fine," Hank conceded, "but it isn't like you not to pursue someone you're clearly interested in. You did tell us you wanted something more substantial in a relationship."

He couldn't deny the validity of Hank's words. Hank, Braden and Gabriel knew him so well. They were always able to see straight through him and all the way down to the parts of him he didn't always like to share with the world. He had no doubt they knew he'd been feeling alone lately.

There wouldn't be any harm in approaching Ella this evening. They were friends after all. He'd been a bit surprised when she had turned down his offer for a ride into town tonight. He had been looking forward to spending more time in her company. He let out a sigh. It was silly for him to be disappointed about something so trivial, yet he couldn't deny how he felt. The car ride would have provided another opportunity to get to know her. Despite his doubts about Ella, he wanted to find out more about her life in Flagstaff and all the small details about her likes and dislikes. Was red her favorite color? Did she envision living out the rest of her days here in Owl Creek? What type of music did she enjoy?

Even though all of his instincts were warning him to steer clear of Ella, he couldn't deny he felt a strong pull in her direction. He vacillated between believing she was hiding something terrible in her past and thinking she was some kind of wonderful. One way or the other, he intended to find out which one was the truth.

"They say the moon is bigger here in Alaska."

Isabelle turned around at the sound of Connor's voice. Although she had glimpsed him from across the way, nothing compared to seeing him up close. Dressed in a pair of dark colored jeans and a navy blue parka that almost matched his eyes, Connor looked casual yet rugged. For the millionth time since she'd arrived in Owl Creek, Isabelle wondered how he had managed to stay single. No doubt it was by choice. She didn't think many women could resist him.

He grinned down at her. "And brighter."

Isabelle felt a smile tugging at the corners of her mouth. "I won't argue with you on that, although I've always heard that the moon is the same size regardless of where you are in the world."

"Rule number one. As a new resident of Owl Creek, you shouldn't question town folklore."

Isabelle laughed. "I see." She held up her mittened hands. "I promise not to ever question Alaskan lore again."

"So, are you having a good time?"

"So far it's been a really fun night. I've never been part of a small-town community before, so it's quite interesting to see how everyone comes together for an event."

"Owl Creekians are friendly, if a bit nosy. Don't be surprised if you're asked about your great-grandmother's little sister's second husband."

She burst out laughing. "Owl Creekians? Is that really a thing? You're kidding, right?"

Connor folded his arms across his chest. "O ye of little faith. I'll have you know that one of my ancestors, Barnabus North, came up with that particular name for the townsfolk."

"B-Barnabus?" Isabelle sputtered, devolving into a fit of the giggles. Unable to stop herself, she ducked her head and continued laughing. "I'm so sorry for laughing at your ancestor, but that name sounds a million years old."

"Thanks a lot. That's my middle name," Connor said, his expression shuttered.

"Woops!" Isabelle raised a hand to cover her mouth. "I'm really putting my foot in my mouth tonight, aren't I?"

A sly smile began to spread across

his face. "Gotcha. I'm just teasing you. I was named after my father. Connor Nathaniel North."

"I like it," she said. "It's a bit more distinguished than Barnabus."

"Hey! Leave Barnabus alone. He was a very distinguished town founder. Just ask Beulah. She happens to be coming this way."

When she turned in the direction of Connor's gaze, Isabelle instantly spotted Beulah, resplendent in a peony pink ensemble. She was walking alongside an older man, who Isabelle assumed was her husband. Another couple was with them, holding hands and making a beeline toward Connor.

Beulah's voice rang out as she greeted her. "Ella! You came! I'm so glad you decided to join us."

"Good to see you as well, Beulah. That color looks lovely on you," Isabelle said.

"That's what I told her," the older gentleman said as he reached out to take Beulah's hand. "I'm Jennings North, Beulah's husband. I've heard a lot about you, Ella. All good things of course." He stuck his hand out and shook hers with vigor. "Welcome to Owl Creek, my dear."

"Thank you," she murmured, surprised to discover he knew who she was. It made her happy to know Beulah had spoken about her in a positive light. She thought Beulah and Jennings just might be the most adorable couple in town.

"These are my parents, Willa and Nate," Connor said, nodding in the other couple's direction. "This is Ella Perez. She came to Owl Creek by way of Arizona to work for us."

Connor's parents looked like they had just stepped out of a healthy Alaskan living ad. Willa bore a striking resemblance to Sage, although her eyes were a bright blue while Sage's were brown. They shared similar features and nearly identical noses. Willa was a petite woman who was dwarfed next to her tall husband. Nate North was just as handsome as his son. With his full head of dark hair and an athletic physique, he appeared quite youthful. Both were smiling in her direction, which immediately calmed her unease at meeting so many people all at once.

"Thank you for coming to work for North Star Chocolates," Nate said, his eyes full of warmth. "We're always grateful for fresh ideas and innovations."

"You're a lovely addition to Owl Creek," Willa gushed. She sent Connor a pointed look, which caused Isabelle to squirm a little bit. It was clear Connor's mother also appeared to have her matchmaker hat on. What was it with small Alaskan towns and people feeling the need to pair people up?

After exchanging pleasantries, they

heard an announcement through the loudspeaker that the dog mushing event would be starting soon. Isabelle found herself swept up in the crowd as everyone moved toward another area of the woods. For a moment it was a bit disorienting, until she felt Connor reach for her hand. Although she sensed he was simply ensuring she wasn't left behind, it was hard to deny how good it felt to have his hand around hers. It gave her a feeling of safety, as if Connor was protecting her from harm. She knew it wasn't romantic, but for a moment Isabelle imagined what it might be like to hold hands with Connor for real.

Stop dreaming about things that won't ever come to pass. It's a complete waste of time. She needed to be firmly rooted in reality.

By the time they reached the area where the mushers were located with their sled dogs, a large crowd had assembled. There was a buzz of excitement in the air.

"What exactly are we going to see?" Isabelle asked. It was slightly embarrassing, but what she knew about dog mushing would easily fit on a postage stamp.

"This is just a demonstration of how dog mushers and their teams perform. They're all going to race along the trail and back to give us an idea of what the longer races look like and how the dogs work as a team to get the job done," Connor explained. "We're raising money tonight to go toward shelter dogs."

"That's a wonderful cause. My family had a Great Dane for twelve years. She was a shelter dog. Her name was Daisy, and she was amazing."

"Great Danes are a handful, much like huskies. Bear keeps me on my toes."

"Yes, they are, but Daisy was a sweetheart. We lost her a few years ago. I still miss her."

"Sounds like you might be in the market for a shelter dog. The vet clinic is doing adoptions all month, just in case you're interested."

Adopting a dog! The idea of doing so hadn't even crossed her mind, although she knew it would do wonders for her loneliness. But what if she had to abruptly leave Owl Creek and move to another location? There was no telling how many different towns she might relocate to. Would it be difficult for a pet to be moved around so much if the need arose?

Isabelle shrugged. "It's something to think about," she said, not wanting to give up on the idea so soon. She would love to have a stable life where owning a dog was possible. Maybe she really could put roots down in Owl Creek without having to look over her shoulder all the time. Perhaps it was possible to live a normal life.

Connor pointed toward one of the mushers. "See the guy in the front wearing the red parka? That's Ace Reynolds. He's an exceptional dog musher," Connor said. "One of the best."

"I heard he grew up here in Owl Creek."

"He sure did. Folks here in town are awfully proud of him. He's going to compete in the Iditarod this March."

Isabelle wrinkled her nose. "The Iditarod? It sounds familiar, but I have to confess that I don't know anything about it."

He winked at her. "As a born and bred Alaskan, I've grown up on it." He let out a chuckle. "The Iditarod is a yearly sled dog race that stretches from Anchorage to Nome. It takes place over the course of eight days or so. It's pretty intense and only for those who are dedicated to the craft. When I was a kid, I wanted so badly to be a dog musher and compete in the Iditarod. Ace was born into it. Both his father and his grandfather competed, so I guess one could say it's in his blood. He's spent so much of his life training and raising the pups. I can't really imagine him doing anything else."

"Are the dogs safe?" she asked. "It's hard to imagine them racing in such a cold climate. Or for such long stretches of time."

"You'll never meet anyone as passionate about dogs as Ace. He treats all of them very well. They're his family."

"That's good to know," Isabelle said, her heart warming at his words.

"These guys are the best of the best," Connor said. "It's a pretty tight-knit group. Some are them are retired, but a few, like Ace, are still competing. It can be very lucrative, but mushers like Ace aren't in it for the paycheck."

Isabelle nodded. Connor was giving

her quite an education. It was an interesting sport with a rich history in Alaska.

"I think they're getting ready to begin," Connor said, pointing toward the starting line. "The teams are going to go two at a time."

Isabelle turned back toward the action as a horn began to blow and a voice announced that the event was about to begin. Since Connor had given her the background on Ace, her eyes were trained on him and his team. When it was his turn to race, the crowd noisily cheered him on, distinguishing him as the clear favorite in the lineup.

As Ace and his team came flying down the path, the noise from the crowd was deafening. A feeling of exhilaration gripped her. The speed and finesse of the mushers and their dogs were spectacular. With the wind blowing in her hair and a fierce chill in the air, Isabelle almost felt as if she was riding on the sled herself. It was no small wonder why this sport was so popular and drew such large crowds. It was an invigorating event, one she never could have experienced back home.

As all the dog mushers crossed the finish line, loud applause broke out among the crowd. Isabelle joined in, clapping enthusiastically.

"That was really incredible," she said.

"There's nothing quite like the first time you see it." Connor flashed her a smile. "It's the official sport of Alaska. Cool, huh?"

"I had no idea," she admitted. "But it makes sense. I can't think of a more thrilling event to watch."

"It's pretty cool seeing it through your eyes." Connor's own eyes twinkled as he looked down at her. His voice injected a feeling of coziness into their conversation. For a moment she almost forgot that they were at a public place and surrounded by an entire community. Everything else faded away.

Was Connor flirting with her or simply being nice? Did it even matter, considering the albatross hanging around her neck? For all intents and purposes she wasn't a free woman. Her past in Miami shadowed her every single day. It never let her forget her limitations.

"I'm really happy to be here," she said lamely, wishing she could simply let loose and go with the flow. But she couldn't, and anger rose up inside of her. She had witnessed a brutal murder that had put her own life in jeopardy. And now, because of it, she had to steer clear of the one man in all of Alaska who made her feel as if good things might be coming her way.

Connor stayed where he was, mere inches away. "If you're hungry we can check out the food truck. They serve a mean gumbo if you want to ward off the chill in the air. There's also a meltin-your-mouth chocolate bread to satisfy even the biggest sweet tooth." His smile served as an invitation. "What do you say?"

She should make an excuse and get as far away from Connor as possible. Perhaps she could tell him she needed to check in with Lissa about what time she wanted to leave the event. But she was hungry and the fare sounded scrumptious. A myriad of thoughts raced through her mind. Before she could rein herself in, Isabelle blurted out, "I'd love to check out the food truck. I haven't eaten since this morning and my stomach has been grumbling so loudly it sounds like a grizzly bear."

"Well, that sounds serious. We better do something about that right away," Connor replied. He held out his arm, and she looped hers through it as they headed off in the direction of the food truck. Although Isabelle knew she was heading into dangerous territory by spending time alone with Connor, she couldn't seem to help herself. He drew her in with the force of a magnet. Just for tonight she was going to enjoy herself with him, secure in the knowledge that it was only a moment in time. When tomorrow morning rolled around, Isabelle would revert back to her plan to stay away from him.

Getting close to a man like Connor would only make her life in the Witness Protection Program way more complicated. As it was, Isabelle felt as if she was trying to keep her head above water with one arm tied behind her back.

Chapter Eight

Connor tried to avoid the curious stares and whispers of the townsfolk. He could feel dozens of eyes focused on him and Ella as they dug into their food. His love life had always been the subject of much speculation in Owl Creek. Since Ella was a newcomer to town, it added a whole new dynamic to their gossip. While a part of him wanted to shoot them dirty looks, he knew taking the high road was more practical. All of his life Connor had been aware of his position in Owl Creek as a member of the North family. As the future CEO of the town's main industry, it was his responsibility to act in a dignified manner.

"Do I have something on my face?" Ella asked him. A frown line marred her brow.

Connor studied Ella for a moment. She looked pretty perfect as far as he could tell. "Not that I can see. Why do you ask?"

She darted a look around them. "Quite a few people are gawking at me. I thought maybe I had chocolate on my nose or something." She took another bite of the sweet treat, emitting a satisfied sound as she munched on it.

Connor stifled a chuckle. She really had tucked into the chocolate bread, and he relished watching her enjoy it so enthusiastically. Ella seemed to have no idea that the two of them were the object of the town's curiosity. "They're not staring at you. It's the fact that we're together that interests them," he acknowledged with a grimace. "It's kind of a town hobby."

Ella's eyes widened. "Oh. I see," she said in a surprised voice.

"I'm sorry. I know it must be a little awkward, but certain folks in a small town love to speculate if they see two people hanging out." He tamped down his irritation. Connor didn't want Ella to feel uncomfortable or to think that the townsfolk were small-minded gossips.

"I get it," she said. "I grew up with a Brazilian grandmother." She ducked her head and giggled. "She and my great-aunts put me under the microscope my whole life. If I was even spotted with a boy, he was automatically my boy-friend. I understand how this all works, even though it can be frustrating."

"I know they don't mean any harm," Connor said. "Much like your grand-mother and aunts, I imagine. Because you're new in town, they want to know more about you. And—" he paused dramatically "—the whole town wants to marry me off."

Ella let out a surprised sound. "Wow. So they're trying to march you down the aisle, huh?" The corners of her mouth were twitching with amusement. He liked seeing this lighthearted side of her. Perhaps he'd simply been picking up on her nervousness about relocating to Alaska up to this point. Tonight she seemed as if she was coming out of her shell.

"Yes. It's an open secret here in town. It doesn't help that my brother, Braden, is getting hitched soon. You know how that is. People have started to look at me cross-eyed because both my younger siblings have settled down."

"That's a bit of pressure, isn't it?"

Connor shrugged. He didn't want to admit that lately it hadn't been as easy to shrug it off. He spotted Sage, Hank and his niece, Addie, standing across the way. Whenever he was in their presence, Connor wondered what it would be like to fall so deeply in love with someone that you wanted nothing more than to devote your life to that person. He'd never felt anything remotely like that.

"It is, but I suppose it's a bit of a compliment. Everyone in town has known me since the day I was born. They really want me to be happy."

"Aren't you happy now?" Ella asked. She was gazing at him intently, as if she really cared about his welfare.

"I'm very content with my life, but when I see my sister and her family, I wonder how much better things could be," he admitted, jerking his chin in Sage's direction. His sister was holding Addie in her arms while Hank was making her giggle by tickling her. Anyone could see that they were a picture-perfect family. He'd surprised himself by being so honest with Ella. Maybe it was easier to admit something of that nature to someone he didn't know very well. Somehow it took the pressure off.

"They do look blissful," Ella said. "Their little girl is precious. She's the spitting image of her daddy."

"That's my niece, Addie. When Sage met Hank, he was a single father, so my sister became a mother when they got married. She fell in love with Hank and got Addie as a beautiful bonus."

"They're such a sweet family. Sage looks like she's a great mom to Addie. She's so loving and attentive. And a schoolteacher to boot. She's like the Mary Poppins of mothers."

The image of his sister swinging down from the sky with an umbrella brought a smile to his face. Connor shifted his gaze in Sage's direction. "She really is incredible, isn't she? It's been amazing getting to know her."

Isabelle furrowed her brow. "What do you mean? Shouldn't you already know her? She's your sister."

Connor let out a ragged sigh. "I didn't grow up with her. This is going to sound pretty wild, but she was kidnapped from our home when she was only three months old. She was missing for twenty-five years. We were only reunited with her a short while ago. Thankfully, we've all bonded, but it's been a tough journey."

Isabelle gasped. Clearly she hadn't known about his family's tragedy. Sometimes it seemed to him as if the entire world knew about what had transpired. When Sage had returned to Owl Creek last year it had coincided with the twenty-fifth anniversary of her abduction. As a result, there had been an abundance of media attention. The headlines had broadcast the story of Sage's return all over the country.

"I do recall hearing the news story, but I didn't pay much attention to it at the time. I can't believe that was Sage."

"The woman who stole her from us

actually ended up raising Sage," Connor explained. Although he didn't mind telling Ella about his family's tragic past, it still hurt to discuss it. Jane Duncan, the kidnapper, had passed away last year, but he still harbored anger toward the woman who had perpetrated such a heinous act.

"I imagine something like that would devastate your whole family," Isabelle said. "For the life of me I can't imagine how my own family would have weathered such a storm. A stolen baby must've led to such unimaginable loss and uncertainty."

"It did. The tragedy was never far from us," he acknowledged. "We could be enjoying a wonderful Christmas celebration when it would rear up and bring us all crashing down to reality. Even as a small child I felt it. There was a void in our family that could never be filled until Lily returned."

Isabelle frowned. "Lily?"

"That's what my parents named Sage at birth. By the time she came back to us, she wasn't Lily anymore. The woman who stole her ended up raising her as Sage."

Isabelle made a tutting sound. "The name change must have been a painful reminder of the abduction, although Sage's return is an incredible blessing."

Connor nodded, then bowed his head. "We all prayed for years for her return. I don't think my folks ever gave up hope. God brought her back to Owl Creek so we could make our family complete. Now we can't imagine how we made it through all those years without her being with us. It just feels so natural."

"I'm feeling a bit ashamed of myself," Ella admitted.

"For what?" he asked. He froze for a moment, wondering if she was about to confess something about her past.

"Ever since I met your sister, I've been viewing her as this perfect woman living a storybook existence." She let out a hollow laugh. "In reality she was an abducted child who was separated from her real family for decades. I can't begin to wrap my head around what that knowledge did to her."

"Sage has been through a lot," he acknowledged. "There's no way you could have known about the burdens she's carried. She walks through life radiating positivity. We like to think that God was with her for every step of her journey. He gave her the strength to seek out her family." He shook his head. It still stunned him to reflect on Sage's courage and tenacity.

"She's way more incredible than I realized. And your family is, too. To endure such a devastating loss, then come together the way you've all done is awe-inspiring."

"I'm fortunate to have a really strong family. It took a little convincing to make me accept Sage as being Lily, but she won me over. I think a big part of me didn't want to be crushed if it turned out she wasn't my sister." He let out a brittle laugh. "Every Christmas when I was a kid I used to insist on hanging up a stocking for my baby sister. At first I think it made my parents uncomfortable, but over time it became something special we did to hold her close to our hearts during the holiday season. Not that she was ever far from us. My family always believed she would come home to us."

"Faith," she murmured. "They believed in something they couldn't see or touch."

"Yes," he answered with a nod. "My folks never gave up on the notion that they would be with their Lily again. It taught me so much about holding fast to one's beliefs."

"Your family sounds incredible. I'd give anything to be with mine right now. Don't get me wrong," she quickly added, "I really value the opportunity to stretch my wings by working for your family's company. I suppose I'm just a bit homesick."

Connor heard the catch in Ella's voice, and it threatened to knock him off his feet. There was so much yearning in her voice. It made him ache for her. She sounded vulnerable and a little bit lost.

He needed to take a step back from this woman, because with every moment they spent together she reeled him in more. And Connor wasn't sure he had the wherewithal to put a stop to it. She'd gotten under his skin. All he could think about was getting closer to her when he knew he should be putting distance between them.

The words had slipped past her lips before she could stop herself. Talking about her family was off-limits. She was really talking up a storm tonight and letting things slip that she shouldn't. She prayed Connor didn't ask her any questions. She really didn't want to have to fabricate a story. It was becoming increasingly difficult to justify her lies. It wasn't making her feel any better by telling herself that the WITSEC program and the danger she was in mandated it.

"Invite them to visit. This town will roll out the red carpet for them. Visiting Alaska makes for a nice family getaway." Connor sounded so excited about the possibility of her family visiting.

"That's not possible," she murmured. Their eyes met and Connor's were full of questions. "They're not in my life at the moment," she admitted. The enormity of the situation came crashing over her. Despite being at an event crowded with people, Isabelle was achingly alone. There was no one who would wish her a happy birthday or bring her chicken noodle soup when she was sick.

Tears pooled in her eyes. *Don't cry*, she told herself. Becoming emotional would only draw more questions from Connor. How could she ever explain herself? Isabelle felt moisture on her cheeks. Despite her best efforts, the tears were flowing. Before she knew it, he was whisking her away from the main area and toward a copse of trees, where they were almost hidden from the festivities.

"Oh, Ella. Please don't cry. It's going to be all right." Connor quickly swallowed up the distance between them and placed his arms around her. She let out a muffled sob against his chest. She felt his hand moving in a circular motion on her back as he murmured soothing words. It was so comforting to be held by him. Isabelle breathed in the woodsy, masculine scent of him. Although she knew it wasn't possible, she didn't want this moment to end. It had been a long time since someone had made her feel safe and protected. For so long now she had been keeping a stiff upper lip and trying to protect herself and her family members from harm. It was nice to take shelter, if only for a little while, in Connor's arms.

After a few moments, Isabelle pulled away from him. Embarrassment made her cheeks feel flushed. She'd been clinging to him as if he was a life pre-server.

"I'm so sorry," she said, dabbing at her eyes with the hem of her sleeve.

Compassion flared in the depths of his blue eyes. "There's no need to apologize. Clearly you love your family. Don't ever give up on making things right with the ones you care about."

She shook her head. "It's not likely to happen. We might never be a part of each other's lives ever again."

He narrowed his gaze as he looked at her. "You're talking to someone who was reunited with his missing sister

after twenty-five years. Don't stop believing that you'll reconcile with them.
With God nothing's impossible."

Even though Connor didn't understand her specific circumstances, his
words were still powerful. Deep down
in her heart, Isabelle believed she would
see her family again, despite what she'd
been told by law enforcement. At moments like this one, it was hard to keep
believing. She prayed on it each and
every day.

Connor was a man of faith, which was
refreshing.

He reached out and smoothed his
gloved hand across her cheek. "You can
talk to me if you need someone to lean
on. I've been told on occasion that I'm
a good listener."

How Isabelle wished she could confide in Connor. Would he understand
what she'd been through after being a
witness to a violent murder? Or would
he be horrified by her involvement in

WITSEC? Either way, she was forbidden from disclosing it to him.

He represented everything solid and upstanding. Connor made her want things she knew were out of her reach. But even though Isabelle understood that Connor didn't factor into her plans, it didn't make her yearning any less.

Perhaps it was wishful thinking, but the way he was looking at her made her believe he was seconds away from kissing her.

Their eyes locked and held. He felt something humming and pulsing in the air between them. Connor knew if he dipped his head down a few inches his lips would be on Ella's. He was tempted to kiss her. He imagined her lips would be soft and inviting. They might just taste like the hot cocoa she'd been drinking. Instead of doing so, he sucked in a deep breath. It was too soon to kiss Ella, despite how badly he wanted to do it. He was still trying to decide if she was hiding something or if he was jumping to conclusions about her.

She was pretty amazing with her compassionate insight into his family's devastation and trauma. And she was opening up more and more. She didn't feel like such a stranger anymore. She'd told him about her family dog even though it had clearly been a painful topic. Maybe he just needed to be more patient.

He didn't know if kissing her would give him clarity, but he was willing to give it a try. *Just go for it*, he told himself. He inched closer and leaned down toward her.

"Connor!"

The sound of his name being called had him instinctively moving away from Ella. He wanted to protect her privacy as well as his own. He didn't have a single doubt in his mind about the town gossip that would ensue if he was spotted kissing Ella. The abrupt interruption made him feel as if someone had poured a bucket of cold water over him. The mood had been ruined.

Much to his surprise, his grandparents were standing a few feet away in the clearing.

"Beg our pardons for the interruption." Beulah sent a pointed look in her husband's direction. "I daresay we have bad timing."

"I'll say," Connor mumbled under his breath. Disappointment washed over him now that the moment had slipped through his fingers.

He darted a glance at Ella. Her cheeks were flushed. Instinct told him it had nothing to do with the frosty temperature. The almost kiss hung in the air between them. He was trying to pay attention to the conversation with his grandparents, but his thoughts kept veering to Ella's kissable pink lips. "We wanted to pass along a message to Ella,"

Jennings said sheepishly. "Sorry about the intrusion."

"No worries," Connor said, placing his hand on his grandfather's shoulder. He couldn't quite put his finger on it, but Jennings looked so much more vital these days. He had been a virtual shut-in after the kidnapping of his grandchild. Only recently had he begun to venture out into the world. Connor felt gratified that he had rebounded so well.

"Ella, the young lady who drove you over here tonight had a medical emergency," Beulah explained. "She was covered in hives."

"Oh, no," Ella said, her face crumpling. "What happened?"

"It seems Lissa had an allergic reaction to something she ate," Jennings explained. "She had to leave so she could get an EpiPen shot at the clinic."

Ella raised a hand to her throat. "That's so scary. She brings one in to work with her every day. Is she going to be all right?"

Beulah patted her on the shoulder. "She's in good hands. One of the town's most eligible bachelors stepped in and drove her to the clinic after Rachel Lawson looked her over. I'm wondering if God is trying to push those two together." Beulah's wide grin threatened to take over her entire face. Connor arched an eyebrow in her direction. Sometimes his grandmother's matchmaking goals were a bit over-the-top.

"Grandmother, let's focus on Lissa's health rather than her social life," Connor said.

Beulah sent him a surprised look. "I apologize if I sounded insensitive, but I have a very good feeling about those two."

Jennings reached out and clasped his wife's hands in his own. "You always do, my dear. You always do."

Beulah had a habit of matchmaking,

but her attempts at bringing couples together had a dismal success rate. Not a single one of her matches had even come close to being a successful couple. And yet she persisted.

"Your heart is in the right place, Beulah," Ella said. Connor could tell Ella's comment pleased his grandmother. She was practically beaming from the praise.

"Let me take you home, Ella," Connor offered. "I think the event is winding down."

Ella finally glanced over at him. She'd been studiously avoiding his gaze ever since his grandparents had shown up. "Thanks. I'd appreciate it. I'm going to call Lissa later to make sure she's all right," Ella added.

"How kind of you," Beulah said. "Please keep us posted."

"I will," Ella said. "She's a real sweetheart."

As they walked as a foursome out into

the main area of the town green, Connor noted that the crowd had thinned considerably. Although he'd wanted to catch up with his old friend Ace, a general scan of the area indicated he may have already departed.

Connor, along with Ella, said goodnight to his grandparents and swiftly made his way over to his truck. He'd parked it on the street right by the Sheriff's office. Once they were both inside the vehicle, Connor turned on the radio in the hopes of erasing the tension that hung in the air.

Ella hadn't said two words to him in the last ten minutes. He wondered whether she was simply worried about Lissa or pondering the fact that he'd almost kissed her. If it was the latter, Connor had no way of knowing whether his kiss would have been well received. For all he knew she might not have been receptive to it. Maybe his grandparents had rescued him from embarrassment.

Perhaps not kissing Ella had been for the best, considering his reservations about her. It wouldn't be wise to go down a romantic road with all these questions about her that continued to crop up. He kept telling himself that he wanted something steady in his personal life. It wouldn't be wise to go down that road with someone whom he wasn't sure he could trust.

Secrets had a way of coming out from the shadows into the light. His own life had taught him that valuable lesson, and it wasn't likely he would forget it anytime soon.

Chapter Nine

Isabelle gazed out of the window as the Alaskan scenery flitted by her car window. A brilliant moon still hung in the sky, surrounded by dozens of twinkling stars. A graceful snowy owl swooped over the branches of a tree, causing Isabelle to let out a gasp of wonder. She had never seen one in person before, and it was a majestic sight. There were so many things she was experiencing in Alaska that she hadn't been exposed to before now. With each passing day, Isabelle was falling more and more in love with the little town of Owl Creek.

Although she had never imagined ever calling it home, it now felt like one. It was a bittersweet realization, since she still yearned for Miami and the people she had left behind.

For the most part, the car ride home with Connor had been filled with awkward silences. Was Connor thinking about the fact that they'd almost shared a kiss? Probably not. Most likely it had been an impulsive act on his part, soon to be forgotten. Men didn't tend to analyze things the way women did.

A smile twitched at her lips at the memory of Beulah and Jennings when they'd interrupted them. Both had appeared sheepish, stunned and incredibly embarrassed. If she hadn't felt so awkward in the moment, Isabelle might have laughed out loud.

As Connor pulled into her driveway, Isabelle took a moment to drink in the coziness of her new abode. A single light shone from inside, lending the house an inviting warmth. There was another light by her front porch that served as a welcoming beacon. It gave her an added sense of security.

She turned toward Connor. "Thank you for bringing me home. Rusty is dropping off my truck in the morning, so I won't need a ride to work anymore." She looked up at him, suddenly feeling a bit bashful. More than ever, she now had an awareness of him as a man. A ruggedly handsome one at that. "I appreciate your kindness. It made things a lot easier for me."

"You're welcome," Connor said. "But I should be thanking you. Driving you made my days more interesting by far. I enjoyed all of our chats." The way he grinned at her made her limbs tremble. She took a slow, steadying breath. The more time she spent in his presence, the more she was tempted to toss her vow of staying away from him out of the window. Who wouldn't want to spend time with him? What woman wouldn't want to be kissed by Connor North?

"That's sweet of you to say, but I'm still grateful. Good night, Connor," she said, quickly opening the door and stepping down before he could come around and open it for her. She heard Connor's voice bidding her good-night, and she turned around to wave before making her way across her snowy walkway to the front door. Once she was inside, she peeked out the window to see Connor slowly driving away. Clearly he'd waited until she was safely in her home before taking off. A true gentleman.

She let out a sigh. Being around him was like sneaking a chocolate from a candy box that she knew she wasn't supposed to eat. In the world of confections, Connor was a truffle—unique, bold and memorable. If only things were different. If only she could be Isabelle rather than Ella.

Tonight they had almost shared a kiss.

If Beulah and Jennings hadn't interrupted them, she was certain it would have happened, even if it would have been too soon.

A part of her had been relieved that they hadn't kissed, while another piece of her yearned to share a tender moment with him. Although she had never had a shortage of boyfriends, Isabelle couldn't ever remember feeling this way before. Excited. Nervous. She cared about him way more than she ever wanted to admit. Sharing even brief snatches of time in his presence lifted her up.

But there would be no more rides to and from work with Connor now that her truck had been fixed. Not sharing that special time with him would be a huge loss for her.

Connor was in a league of his own. He was funny and easy to talk to. He was charming, but not in a cheesy way. He'd made her laugh so hard her stomach hurt, telling her stories about Beulah and growing up in the North family. It hurt to know how badly they must have all suffered due to Sage's abduction. Although Connor didn't know it, they'd each gone through trauma that resulted in lasting scars. Connor and his family had already endured the worst kind of pain imaginable as a result of lies and deception.

It had been heartwarming to see Sage, Hank and their child bonded as a loving family. Although it reminded her of everything she'd left behind and all the dreams she would have to forgo for her own future, it hadn't made her want to curl up in a ball and cry. It had given Isabelle hope. Maybe one day she could move past all the trauma from having witnessed a murder. Perhaps being in the Witness Protection Program wasn't the end for her.

Please, Lord, help me stay positive so I can have the future I've always dreamed of having. I need to have faith in You and the promise of a new day. I need to keep believing even when others tell me my dreams are not going to come to fruition.

Earlier today she had resisted the strong urge to reach out to her family by phone. She'd ached to hear the sound of their voices and to let them know that she was doing all right. Isabelle worried about her parents and the toll the entire situation had taken on them. Her family had no idea that WITSEC had relocated her to Alaska. Disclosing such information would have risked her status in the program and potentially brought danger into her life. It would have erased all the efforts of Marshal Kramer and his team to create a new identity for her in Owl Creek.

Her loved ones were safer not knowing anything about her location, even though it hurt to feel so disconnected from them. She drew strength from her family and the Lord. God was still beside her even though she was all alone. It didn't stop her heart from aching, but He sustained her as nothing else could.

It had taken all the courage in the world not to give in and make the call to her family. All of her life she'd played by the rules. Working at the night club had been her first act of rebellion, one she'd lived to dearly regret. Her parents hadn't approved of Club Oasis or its drinking and party atmosphere. Now she had to live with the consequences of her decision. It wouldn't be fair to get involved with anyone and have him bear her burdens.

Connor's handsome face flashed before her eyes. Just remembering the way their eyes had locked earlier caused her pulse to skitter. She liked Connor North way more than she wanted to. He was growing on her and she was powerless to stop it. He represented all of the things she had once dreamed of in a romantic partner. But he was off-limits.

Connor had already been put through enough turmoil in his life. By becoming involved with him, Isabelle would only be dragging him into another terrible situation filled with half-truths and lies.

The next morning, Connor drove to the factory all by himself. It felt strange not to have Ella beside him in the passenger seat, even though he'd been doing the ride solo for many years before she'd arrived in Owl Creek. Suddenly, it felt like something was missing. It didn't take a rocket scientist to figure out it was Ella's sweet presence. The knowledge hit him squarely in the face. His feelings for Ella were growing incrementally each day.

Connor hit the brakes as a caribou loped across the road roughly fifty feet ahead of him. He took a moment to admire the graceful creature. He hoped Ella didn't run into any animals on her way into work. The last thing she needed was to have another wreck or be frightened at the sight of an animal.

It's not your problem, he reminded himself. Ever since Ella arrived in town, Connor had made it his business to look out for her. As a result, he'd veered way over the line with regards to keeping a distance from her. Despite his gut instincts warning him about the newcomer to town, he'd continued to befriend her. Last night he'd almost kissed her!

Who was he kidding? he asked himself. Kissing Ella would have been amazing, even if he still harbored doubts about her past. It would have been a moment of discovery between them. Maybe then he could have figured out if his interest in her was reciprocated. As it was, he'd just been left with more doubts.

He felt a funny sensation in his chest at the thought of merely being friends with Ella. It wasn't what he wanted, but he couldn't be anything more than her friend with so many doubts still swirling around regarding the secrets she was keeping.

He didn't feel like his usual self as he made his way through the building. Although many employees called out to him as he walked by, Connor could only nod his head. Things couldn't go on this way. He needed to completely forget about growing their friendship into anything more meaningful.

Connor closed his office door behind him and settled behind his desk. For the next few hours he focused on work without talking to any of his colleagues. When something was bothering him, Connor tended to go inward. He'd always been this way, going back to childhood. Not even Gabe or Hank could penetrate his mood.

When a knock sounded on his door, Connor couldn't stifle his annoyance.

"Come in," he said gruffly. He didn't

really care who was on the other side of the door. At the moment he was feeling grumpy and completely out of sorts.

"Well, good morning to you, too." At the sound of his grandmother's voice, Connor lifted his head. She was standing in the doorway dressed in a bright blue pantsuit that only Beulah could get away with. And for the life of him, he couldn't be aggravated when she was nearby.

"Morning, Grandmother." He glanced at the clock on his desk. "It's almost afternoon, though. I don't know where the time is going."

She was gazing at him with a look of compassion in her eyes. "I can tell you have a lot on your mind, but I won't pry," Beulah said.

"I'm just having an off day," he said. There was no way he was going to talk to Beulah about Ella. The last thing he needed was to have his grandmother meddling in his personal life.

"All right," she said. "I'll take what you're saying at face value."

"What's up? You look like you're about to burst. Has something happened?" Connor asked. He knew this woman well. She was overjoyed about something and it showed.

"We've picked our latest employee of the week," she announced. "We printed up a certificate of distinction, and we're giving her a gift card and flowers."

"Who got it? I'm sure it'll brighten their day."

"It's Ella. I was wondering if you wanted to stop by the chocolate shop and tell her in person. She'll be thrilled to hear the news, I imagine, and get the recognition."

Hearing that Ella was being hailed by the company uplifted Connor's dark mood. It gave him a kick just thinking about her reaction to the news. But he didn't want to be near her right now. It was still confusing trying to figure out how he was going to stay solely in the friend zone with Ella. Steering clear of her might make it easier.

"Uh, I actually have a call later on. I can't do it, although I know the award will make her really happy."

Beulah appeared crestfallen. Her smile vanished and her brows knitted together. "I thought you and Ella were getting along like a house on fire, judging by last night." She fluttered her eyes.

He should have known his grandmother wouldn't let what she'd witnessed last night go by without a comment. It wasn't in her nature. She had a tendency to meddle in the lives of her family members. He knew it came from a place of love, but at the moment it only added to his frustration. "I'm not even going to respond to that. There's nothing romantic between us. We're just friends."

Beulah arched an eyebrow. "That's

even more reason to be the one to tell her the good news. It won't be the same if I send one of my employees over there who doesn't know Ella. It won't be as meaningful."

"It can't be helped," he said tersely. With every word Beulah uttered, Connor felt his willpower faltering. He would love to head over to the chocolate shop and surprise Ella with something encouraging like employee of the week. Was he being selfish by only considering his own feelings? Truthfully, he was protecting himself. He was getting in way too deep with his feelings for Ella.

"It might be a nice pick-me-up," Beulah said. "Not just for Ella, but for you as well. Get outside, take a nice walk in the fresh air. Give someone some good news. It might cheer you up."

Connor let out a sigh. He knew when Beulah sounded like this she wasn't going to give up until she got her way. He might as well save himself a colossal headache and agree to do as she'd requested. No matter how he tried to stay away from Ella, forces kept pushing him in her direction. He just had to stay strong. Connor would present the news to Ella as a friend. Nothing more.

"All right. I'll swing by the shop. Happy now?"

"I'm always happy when people do the right thing," she answered in a singsong voice. "Let me go back to my office and bring you the certificate and the goodies." Beulah sailed out the door with a spring to her step. She returned a few minutes later with a canvas bag. The bouquet of flowers was poking out of the top.

Before he changed his mind, Connor put his coat and boots on in preparation for the walk to Main Street. As he strode along, he had to admit that getting a dose of the crisp Alaskan air was good for him.

When he entered the store, Connor immediately noticed a commotion going on inside the normally orderly place of business. Kids were scattered everywhere. Connor's gaze immediately settled on Ella. She was bent over at the waist talking to a little girl whose lip was stuck out in a dramatic pout. Ella was speaking in a low voice, and although he couldn't hear what she was saying, he knew it was soothing. The little girl leaned in for a hug and wrapped her arms around Ella before darting off to join some pals. When Ella stood up, their eyes met across the shop. A hint of a smile played around her lips at the sight of him. That simple act buoyed him. Connor made his way to her side.

"Connor! What brings you here?" Ella asked. "As you can see, this place is jumping today with first-graders. Sage arranged a tour for her students." Ella's eyes twinkled. "Giving chocolate samples to six-year-olds is a bona fide way to make them happy."

Connor looked around the shop at all the happy little faces. He let out a chuckle. "Sage might regret giving them candy before they head back to class."

Sage and another teacher were doing their best to quiet the kids down to a dull roar. His sister looked over and sent an apologetic look in Ella's direction. In return, Ella simply smiled.

"Only one piece of chocolate per child," Ella said. "That's the rule."

"A wise decision," he said. "I'm a big fan of the stuff, but too much of it can make children bounce off the walls."

Ella grinned. "That's what my sister always says." Once the words were out of her mouth, Ella's expression changed. All the light faded from her eyes, replaced by a somber expression.

Connor could see the sadness emanating from her eyes. He knew the source of it was homesickness. Braden had left Owl Creek for three years as a self-imposed penance for the accident that had killed Piper's father. He'd later confided in Connor about the deep sense of isolation he'd experienced due to missing his family members and friends. Connor imagined Ella felt the same way. He didn't want to ply her with questions about her sister or do anything to accentuate her sorrow.

"I came to ask you if you wanted to grab lunch." Connor blurted out the invitation. The words had poured out of his mouth like water from a faucet. Lunch? Where had that idea come from? All he'd been planning to do was to deliver the good news to Ella and then head back to the factory. It wasn't like him to veer so wildly off course. Evidently, this woman brought it out in him.

"I'd love to go to lunch," Ella said, smiling at him as she answered. "If you can wait fifteen minutes or so until Sage's class leaves."

"I can wait," he said with a nod. "I'll get out of your hair until the kids clear out." Connor beat a fast path to the door, stepping outside into the frosty air. As a cold breeze whipped across his face, Connor let it wash over him. All of a sudden he had no actual clue as to what he was doing. He wasn't used to acting so spontaneously. He'd always thought things out and acted in a deliberate manner.

What am I doing? Sharing a meal with Ella wasn't taking a step back as he'd vowed to do. He was getting in deeper and deeper without an exit strategy.

Sitting across from Connor at the Snowy Owl Diner was an unexpected development in Isabelle's day. To say she'd been surprised by his unannounced appearance at the chocolate shop would be a major understatement.

Try as she might, Isabelle couldn't convince herself that she should have turned his invitation down. Being around him made her feel good. And it was flattering that someone like Connor would ask her out to lunch when most of the women in town would jump at the chance. Working at the shop gave her an opportunity to listen to the chatter of the customers and her staff members. Connor North was a hot commodity in Owl Creek. From the sounds of it, he had dated prolifically, yet he hadn't ever had a steady love interest.

Frankly, his romantic history in town was none of her business. He was free to date half the town if he so desired. This wasn't a date! It was merely a simple lunch between friends.

Isabelle focused on the menu, even though she knew exactly what she was ordering. The salmon cakes with a cup of crab stew would make for a divine lunch. Looking at Connor across the table was akin to falling into the void. Why did he have the most piercing blue eyes? And the steadiest gaze. It always made her feel as if he could see straight through her. She shivered at the idea that he knew she was a woman harboring secrets.

By the time the waitress had arrived at their table and taken their orders, she and Connor had started up a conversation about the best places to spot rare species of birds in Owl Creek. Isabelle was really intrigued by the idea of birdwatching in Alaska. If anyone had told her a year ago she would be contemplating such an activity, she would have laughed herself silly.

Isabelle took a long sip of her hot cocoa. It felt nice to be inside and away from the cold. She still hadn't gotten used to being bundled up all the time and the frequent snowstorms. Perhaps years from now she would be acclimated to Alaska.

"So, I actually brought you out to lunch to celebrate."

"Celebrate what?" she asked. He'd completely piqued her curiosity. It was flattering to think he'd chosen her as a companion to revel in good news.

He reached into his bag and pulled out a folder. Connor handed it to her with a flourish.

"Congratulations," he said. "You've been chosen as employee of the week by Beulah. That's your certificate. I've also got flowers and some goodies you can take with you." He handed her the bag he'd carried in. "She's really proud of the hard work and extra hours you've put in."

"Me?" she asked, feeling incredulous. "But I haven't worked for the company for very long."

"Well, what can I say? Beulah makes those distinctions and she really sang your praises. It isn't easy working for the North Star Chocolate Company when you don't have a background in chocolate. You've made a tremendous effort to learn your craft. It hasn't gone unnoticed."

Warmth flooded her cheeks. It was an exhilarating feeling to know that she'd made a difference. She had always been a hard worker, but she hadn't always been proud of her work environment at Club Oasis. This was different from any other job she'd ever held. Isabelle felt a deep sense of pride in working for such a prestigious chocolatier.

"I… I don't know what to say." Her eyes moistened with emotion. This time the tears stemmed from a joyful place. It was a wonderful feeling to finally be happy about something after a long period of being fearful and uncertain. Perhaps this was a milestone. Maybe she was finally stepping out into the light.

Connor reached over and placed his hand over hers. "Savor the moment. You've earned it."

Isabelle nodded. It was hard for her to toot her own horn, but she knew that the recognition from Beulah was a game changer. Ever since she'd arrived in Owl Creek, she had been afraid to be herself. It was almost as if she'd been walking around with a costume on this entire time. The employee of the week distinction was an acknowledgment of her strong work ethic. Even though she'd been raised to be humble, Isabelle wanted to bask in Beulah's kudos for a few moments. It made her feel as if she was on top of the world. Something told her it might not last, since her life under the Witness Protection Program was stressful and unpredictable.

She was feeling a bit emotional after Connor's news about her employee of the week award. All of the employees she worked with at the store were hard-working and diligent. Compared to the late nights she'd spent working at Club Oasis in Miami, her position at North

Star Chocolates was delightful. She was now working normal hours as opposed to heading into work at night and not getting off until the wee hours of the morning. And she always felt safe.

When the waitress returned with their food, Isabelle found her appetite had lessened due to her excitement. She took a few bites of her salmon cakes while Connor voraciously tucked in to his pollack, french fries and coleslaw.

"You better pinch me because it feels like I'm dreaming," Ella said.

Connor reached out and gently plucked the skin by her wrist. "There. I did it. And it doesn't change the fact that you earned this distinction. Kudos, Ella."

She raised a hand to her cheeks. Warmth flooded her face. She wasn't sure if it was because of his compliments or his close proximity. It was getting harder and harder to ignore that

Connor North was dangerous to her equilibrium.

"So, do they hang up a photo of me in the chocolate shop? I can't wait to be queen for a day," she teased.

"Yeah, we like to make a big deal out of it. We're going to shout it from the rooftops. We'll put your picture up in the store and at the factory. Then we'll place it on the company website and add it to our monthly newsletter. You'll be famous by the time this month is done." He let out a low chuckle.

"It's going on the internet?" Ella asked, swallowing past the lump in her throat. All of a sudden her heart began beating a fast rhythm within her chest. *No!* she wanted to scream. She couldn't run the risk of her face being plastered on the internet. Although it was unlikely the people who wanted to harm her would ever see it, she wasn't willing to take a chance. If Burke and his cohorts got a lead on her whereabouts, they wouldn't hesitate to track her down in Owl Creek. The very thought of it made her shudder.

"Maybe. I'm not really sure," Connor answered. "Hey. What's wrong? Aren't you happy about this?"

"O-of course I am. I just don't like all the attention that comes with it." She bit her lip as her mind raced with how to explain her sudden wariness about the distinction. She had been over the moon about being employee of the week until discovering there might be online fanfare.

Connor frowned. "You're confusing me. I hope you understand this is a good thing. You aren't trying to hide your light under a bushel, are you?"

She shook her head. "In what way?"

"It's something my grandfather used to say. Basically it means don't hide your talents or abilities. Let them shine. The Bible verse comes to mind. 'Let your light so shine before men, that they may see your good works.'"

She was familiar with the Bible verse, but Isabelle didn't see herself reflected in it. She wasn't hiding her light. Isabelle was trying to preserve her status in WITSEC by not being exposed.

Isabelle nodded and continued to nibble her meal. At this point it tasted like sawdust. All she felt was a growing sense of dread. She didn't know how she could do this for the long haul. Would she ever be able to sit back and relax without feeling as if a dark cloud was hanging over her head? Would she ever not wake up terrified in the middle of the night? And now, just when things had started to solidify for her in Owl Creek, she was being plunged back into fear, doubt and second-guessing herself.

If her picture was plastered all over the internet, would she need to leave town? She felt a pang in her heart at the idea of packing up and leaving. Where would she go? And how could she leave everything behind?

"I hate to eat and run, but I have a conference call this afternoon." Connor's comment drew her out of her thoughts. She hoped he hadn't noticed her inattention. She'd deliberately stuffed down her feelings regarding her commendation going online. She couldn't afford to make a scene about it or betray her deep concerns. There were already too many instances where she'd acted strangely in his presence. Connor was a smart guy. He'd probably picked up on her odd behavior. It was only a matter of time before he began to question what was going on with her.

She looked at her watch. "Oops. Where did the time go? I need to head back to the shop. Thanks for the lunch invitation. And for giving me such great news."

"Well, thanks for joining me. And again, congratulations. It says a lot about you that you earned this praise." Connor seemed genuinely happy for her.

"It means a lot to me. Please tell Beulah how thrilled I am." Isabelle warmed at the compliment. She did feel proud, and she hoped Connor had been able to see her happiness despite her shattered nerves.

Connor pulled out some bills and plunked them down on the table. He walked with Ella to the exit. As they stood outside, Ella tilted her face upward. Snowflakes were falling gracefully from the sky. If only she could just enjoy this beautiful moment instead of worrying about her status in the Witness Protection Program. She longed to cast all her troubles aside and simply live the way other people did. Without fear or regrets.

"It was very thoughtful of you to come deliver the news in person," she said. "I appreciate it." She had been telling herself all this time she couldn't afford to feel anything for Connor, but at moments like this one her will was being tested. Being with him always made her feel good.

He handed her the bag he'd brought with him. "I like seeing you smile, Ella. It was my pleasure. I hope to see you soon." As Connor strode off in the direction of the factory, Isabelle paused for a moment to admire him. She liked the proud tilt of his head and the way he carried himself. Once he turned the corner and disappeared from view, her mind began to whirl with worry.

She needed to call Jonah immediately. This was definitely an emergency situation that called for her to contact the U.S. Marshal. Her entire cover could be blown if her picture was circulated online. Isabelle dug in the side pocket of her purse and pulled out her cell phone. Jonah had programmed his number into her phone when they'd parted ways. Isabelle walked to the parking lot behind the chocolate shop and made her way to her truck. Once she was inside, she placed the call.

As soon as she heard the familiar voice on the other end, Isabelle spoke into the phone. "Jonah, it's me, Isabelle Sanchez. I don't know what to do! My employer might be uploading my picture online. I might have to leave Owl Creek."

Chapter Ten

Connor looked around the crowded tea
emporium and pondered sneaking out
the back entrance. He felt a bit out of
place with all the frilly lace and velvet cushions. He thought Tea Time was
a wonderful business for Owl Creek,
but he'd never really been tempted to
sit down and indulge in an afternoon
tea party. Connor had to admit that Iris
and the bridal party had created a lovely
ambience.

"How did I get dragged into a bridal
shower?" Connor asked. He turned to

question his brother, who was standing next to him.

"Because you were invited. Just like I was," Braden answered. "And you didn't want to let Piper down. She's the only sister-in-law you're ever going to have."

"I didn't realize these things were now coed." There were a decent number of men who'd showed up for the event. Way more than he'd envisioned. Gabe and Hank were across the room having a disagreement over tea flavors. Since Gabe's mother owned Tea Time, he was an expert on the subject. Hank, on the other hand, adored tea and considered himself a connoisseur.

"Me neither, but I'm making the best of it. Piper deserves a nice surprise."

"Speaking of the blushing bride-to-be, what time is she expected to arrive?" Connor asked, studiously trying to avoid the flirty looks he was receiving from across the room. Lana Travers had been trying to get him to take her out for the last few months. Although she was attractive and sweet, he simply wasn't interested. Now that Ella had arrived in town, he'd lost interest in dating around.

Braden glanced at his watch. "In ten minutes or so. She thinks we're meeting for a romantic high tea."

Connor snickered. "That in itself should make her suspicious. You're not the tea emporium type of guy."

"That's not true!" Braden protested. "Just because I'm into outdoor adventures doesn't mean I can't appreciate the finer things. I'm a Renaissance man."

Just as Connor opened up his mouth to dispute his brother's comment, he spotted Ella walking into the tea shop. She was carrying a gaily wrapped present in her arms. Trudy Miller, Piper's mother, greeted her at the door and whisked her toward the coatroom. Connor stood up straight and smoothed his hair back.

"Has something gotten your attention? You haven't heard a word I said."

He turned back toward Braden. "I'm sorry. What were you saying?"

Braden was shaking his head and chuckling. "She's very pretty. Ella, right?"

"Yes. She really is," he answered, not bothering to pretend as if he hadn't been distracted by Ella's arrival. "I haven't known her very long, but she's different from any woman I've ever met." He felt sheepish admitting it. "I probably sound ridiculous. Most people view me as this perpetual bachelor, don't they? I'm not supposed to have feelings."

"I'm not most people, Connor. I'm your brother. I happen to like this side of you. And I wish more people could see that your greatest asset is that big old heart of yours."

"It's my own fault for always playing it cool. That gets old after a while," he admitted. He couldn't blame others for viewing him in a certain way when he'd earned the title. Now he was hoping to go a different route. Lately, he'd prayed a lot about it, asking God to shoulder him through his journey.

Trust in the Lord with all thine heart; and lean not unto thine own understanding. In all ways acknowledge him, and he shall direct thy paths.

The passage from Proverbs 3:5–6 had been his cornerstone as of late. He'd been reciting it every day without fail.

"Just remember, it's never too late to change," Braden said. "Follow your heart. That's what I did with Piper."

Follow your heart. That's what it boiled down to. His head over his heart. All the doubts he had about Ella had prevented him from pursuing her romantically. But in doing so, wasn't he coming from a place of fear and suspicion? It felt as if he was allowing his own family's tragic past to shape his actions. Just because one person had done a horrible thing didn't mean he should be suspicious of all strangers. Was he biased against Ella because of Sage's kidnapper, a single woman who'd come to town and stolen his baby sister? Was he allowing a twenty-five-year-old tragedy to cloud his judgment?

"You'll figure it out," Braden said, clapping him on the shoulder. "I'm going to check in with Piper just to make sure she's running on schedule." He held up his cell phone as he walked toward a private area.

Just then, Ella walked into the main tearoom wearing a cornflower blue dress and a pair of black heels. She radiated a bright and festive air. She looked over at him and waved, right before heading in his direction.

"Hey, Connor. I'm surprised to see you here."

"Not as surprised as I am to be here," he said with a laugh.

"I've never been to a coed shower,

but I like the idea of it. Why shouldn't your brother share in the revelry?" She looked around. "Should we be getting in position to hide? Sage said this is a surprise party."

"Braden is checking in with Piper. She's supposed to arrive anytime now."

"It was nice of your sister to invite me. I'm afraid I don't know Piper very well. I think Sage felt sorry for me since I'm new in town."

"No, that's not it at all. She was a newbie in town once, so she knows how it feels to be out of the loop. Plus, I saw you hanging out at the dog mushing event with Piper, so you're not strangers. What you might not have realized yet is that you're really not an outsider for very long in Owl Creek. You're part of the fabric of this community now."

A grin broke out on her face. "That's good to hear. It makes me feel better that I decided to come today. I almost chickened out."

"I'm awfully glad you didn't. Seeing you was a nice surprise for me." As soon as the words tumbled off his lips, he wondered if his comment sounded sappy. Or too flirty? Just as Ella opened her mouth to say something, Piper's mother raised the alarm.

"Piper is right around the corner. Everybody hunker down," Trudy shouted.

Everyone began shuffling around and ducking out of sight. Connor found himself crouching down beside Ella behind a table. They were so close together he could smell a sweet aroma emanating from her dark tresses. He could hear the light sound of her breathing. Their faces were so close to one another that Connor could see the light flecks in her brown eyes. From where they were hiding, he could see Braden walking toward the entrance to greet Piper. The room was eerily quiet as Piper walked in and Braden welcomed her with a tender kiss. As soon as Braden led her toward the dining room and uttered the words, "You look lovely," all of the guests popped up and shouted, "Surprise." Piper looked around the room with an expression of utter shock stamped on her face. She then burst into tears. Braden lovingly placed his arm around her as she thanked everyone for gathering in her honor.

Connor looked over at Ella. A look of pure radiance emanated from her. Seeing her so happy and at ease caused a groundswell of emotion to rise up inside him. It was evident she was starting to feel a sense of belonging, despite second-guessing her invitation.

If he hadn't fully realized it before, it was now stunningly obvious. Ella Perez had a hold on him. And for the life of him, he wasn't sure what to do about it.

With the bridal shower tea party in full swing, Ella couldn't think of a time when she'd had more fun celebrating an upcoming wedding. Her cheeks hurt from smiling so much, but she couldn't rein herself in. Being at Piper and Braden's celebration made her feel included. Seeing the couple being celebrated by the whole town was heartwarming.

Connor was one of the good guys, and he deserved far better than a woman who might spend the rest of her life hiding her true identity. Connor came from a strong, loving family who lived their lives out in the open. He wasn't a man who abided secrets. He'd told her as much when he had spoken about Sage's abduction. A man like Connor North wouldn't want to have anything to do with her if he knew she was living a lie.

The other day had been a nerve-racking experience until Connor had later informed her that her picture wasn't going to be placed online on the company website. He'd agreed to only list her name and her award. She couldn't help but feel that he'd sensed her extreme discomfort and made an adjustment. Isabelle had quickly contacted Jonah to update him on the news. Although the U.S. Marshal had clearly been relieved by the update, he'd been very firm in telling her to keep her guard up and to continue to stay alert to any potential situations that might compromise her identity. Getting reassurance from Jonah that she was safe made all the difference in her state of mind. It had allowed her to attend the bridal shower and cast her fears aside, at least temporarily.

At the moment she was trying to enjoy the festivities and bask in the happy vibe in the air. She took a sip of her tea, marveling at the unique taste and the elegant gold-and-pink teacup and saucer. There were so many lovely details here on display. The refreshment table was filled with finger sandwiches, scones, croissants and tarts. A two-tiered cake had been placed in the center of the table. A plentiful assortment of teas sat on another table. Everything was lavishly displayed in soft and inviting colors.

"It's so great to see you here." Ella turned toward Rachel, who was standing alongside her with her mother-in-law in tow. Iris reached out and enveloped Isabelle in a tight hug.

"I'm so glad to see you're making yourself at home," Iris gushed. "There will always be a table for you at Tea Time."

"That's so kind of you to say, Iris. Everything is so beautiful here. I love this lavender tea. I've never had anything quite like it." Isabelle took another sip of the fragrant tea.

"It's also a favorite of mine. We actually have favors with tea packets inside, so you can take some samples home with you," Iris said.

"That's a perfect party favor," Isabelle answered. She looked over at the refreshment table, where Connor was standing with his parents.

"He's a good-looking man, isn't he?" Iris asked, jerking her chin in Connor's direction. She turned her gaze to Isabelle, shooting her a questioning look.

"Umm, yes. He's all right, I suppose," Isabelle said, trying to keep her voice neutral.

She knew how small towns worked. If she raved about Connor's dark good looks, the townsfolk would soon be talking about her and how the new girl in town was crushing on the heir to the North Star Chocolate Company. Her face felt flushed just thinking about how embarrassing it would be if Connor got wind of any chatter. She was supposed to be keeping her head down and maintaining a low profile. Being the subject of matchmaking schemes or gossips wouldn't aid her objective.

"Just all right?" Iris asked in a voice

full of outrage. "Ella, I think you might need glasses. Connor North is Alaskan eye candy."

Rachel playfully swatted at her mother-in-law. "Iris! Stop it. You're incorrigible."

Iris stood up straighter and puffed her chest out. "I might be a woman of a certain age, but there's nothing wrong with my eyesight. He's as single as a dollar bill, Ella. And from the looks of it, he's always ready to mingle. Beulah is hoping he'll settle down and focus on one woman instead of hopping from woman to woman as he's always done."

Isabelle did her best to hide her discomfort. Although Iris clearly adored Connor, she wasn't putting him in the best light. Clearly, Isabelle's impression of Connor had been far from reality.

"He sounds like a player," Isabelle murmured. She shouldn't be surprised. Men who looked like Connor often had their pick of women. It didn't hurt that he hailed from a prominent family and held an executive position at North Star Chocolates.

Rachel none too subtly jabbed Iris in the side. "We don't want Ella to get the wrong idea about Connor. He's a good man."

"Of course he is. It's not his fault he's cut a huge swath through all the women in town. Ever since he was young, he's been the object of every girl in town's affection."

"Umm, hello. Not mine," Rachel interjected. "I always had my eye on a certain pilot."

Iris leaned in and pressed a kiss on Rachel's cheek. "Bless your heart. You sure did. My son is blessed to have you. I should scoot and replenish the refreshments. I'll catch up with you later."

Isabelle felt thankful for Iris and her chatty ways. Iris's intel on Connor made her feel grateful that she hadn't locked lips with Connor the other night.

Clearly, he viewed women as conquests. She felt embarrassed that she'd thought Connor was interested in her. According to Iris, he played the field like a champion. She stuffed down the feelings of disappointment. It would have been an impossible situation between them anyway, but it rankled a little bit to realize she wasn't special in his eyes.

"I wouldn't quite describe Connor the way Iris did," Rachel said, interrupting her thoughts. "My mother-in-law is very opinionated, so I wouldn't take her words to heart. Everyone in Owl Creek adores Connor."

Clearly, Rachel felt an allegiance to Connor, and she didn't want Isabelle to think poorly of him. She appeared to be doing a bit of damage control.

Isabelle shrugged. "It's not my place to judge him. I honestly don't know him that well."

"He's a really good person. I've known

him my entire life," Rachel added. An earnest expression was stamped on her face.

She nodded her head but didn't comment any further. She didn't want to talk about Connor anymore. Iris had dropped a little bombshell on her. It served as a wake-up call and she was still trying to process what she'd learned. His past really wasn't her business, although it did give her perspective.

For the remainder of the party Isabelle did her best to mingle and enjoy the festivities. She participated in a variety of games, even managing to win a round of bridal song trivia. Her prize was a large surprise packet that she couldn't wait to dig into once she got home. It was thrilling, since she never won anything.

Piper made a point to seek her out during the party. Isabelle wasn't expecting to receive a bear hug from the guest of honor, but it reinforced her feelings about the lively bride-to-be. She was just as sweet and kindhearted as Isabelle had imagined. Slowly but surely Isabelle was becoming a part of things here in Owl Creek. She didn't feel quite so lonely anymore. Now, when she walked down Main Street, there were friendly faces who called out to her by name. Customers in the shop asked for her when they came through the doors. Although she still looked over her shoulder from time to time, Isabelle felt safe in her small Alaskan haven. She prayed that her identity was never compromised. She didn't want to be forced to leave town as she'd feared a few days ago.

Fear was still a living, breathing thing inside of her. Would she ever have an aura of peace surrounding her? Or would the past always hang over her head? Isabelle needed to have faith in Jonah and his assurances.

Lord, please give me a spirit of grace

and not fear. I'm so tired of looking over my shoulder and wondering if I'm still in danger. Please lift me up so I can see beyond my anxieties. Bless my future and help me banish the past.

As the party began to wind down, Ella left the main tearoom to gather up her belongings in the coatroom. She'd already said her goodbyes to Piper, Iris, Sage and Rachel. Just as she was putting on her coat, Isabelle felt a slight tap on her shoulder. When she turned around, Connor was standing there.

"Hey. Are you heading out?" he asked.

"Yes," she answered, zipping up her coat before adjusting her hat. "It was a great party, but I'm tired."

"I barely got to talk to you at all," he said.

She shifted from one foot to the other. It wasn't as if she'd been avoiding him, but she hadn't sought him out either. Truthfully, she felt a little self-conscious around him now, based on the information Iris had shared with her. It was ridiculous on her part, considering Connor could never be anything more than a friend.

"Well, the place was packed. All these people must really love Piper and Braden."

Connor nodded. "Everyone enjoys a good love story. They were childhood best friends throughout their lives, so it's all the sweeter that they fell in love."

It was utterly charming. No wonder they were the town's sweethearts. It's what everyone wanted. Marrying your best friend and making a beautiful life together would be a dream come true for most people. A heaviness settled on her chest. Something so wonderful wasn't destined for her. And it was beginning to weigh on her. Isabelle had always been the little girl dreaming of a big wedding filled with family and friends. Most importantly, she had fantasized about marrying a man who brought her joy.

"I'm so happy for them," she said, though her voice sounded wooden to her own ears. She hated feeling this way and wondered when she'd return to her usual upbeat and positive vibe.

"I have to get going," she said, before quickly striding toward the door. She imagined Connor thought her actions were abrupt, but she didn't stop walking at a fast clip until she reached her truck, which was parked down the street. Along the way she breathed in big gulps of the cold air, all the while reminding herself that this too would pass. Surely better days were coming. Every step on her journey would carry her through the darkness. Isabelle prayed she would be strong enough to see it through.

Connor had felt a slight chill in the air as he said his goodbyes to Ella—

and it had nothing to do with the actual temperature. He wasn't sure what he'd done, but instinct told him she was annoyed with him. Perhaps he should have made more of an effort to seek her out at the party, but he'd been worried about smothering her. It was fantastic that she'd been welcomed, but now he was scratching his head about what he'd done wrong. It mattered to him what Ella thought about him. He wasn't the type of man who had ever been overly concerned about the opinion of others, but with this woman everything had been turned upside down.

A half an hour later Connor was helping with the cleanup and still racking his brain to figure out Ella's frosty demeanor. Earlier, she'd been fine. Perhaps he'd stepped over the line with her in some way that made her uncomfortable.

Sage made a beeline in his direction.

"Hey. Have you seen Ella anywhere? I can't seem to find her."

"She left a few minutes ago. You just missed her."

Sage let out a groan. "She left behind her goody bag and the prize package she won. I guess that I could swing by her place tomorrow after Addie's Gymboree class and give it to her."

"I can take it to her if you want. She lives a few minutes down the road from me, so it's not a big deal."

Sage's eyes lit up. "Seriously? That would be fantastic. You're the best, Connor."

"Of course I am," he teased. "I'm still waiting for that favorite brother T-shirt."

Sage put a finger up to her lips. "Shh. We don't want Braden to hear." They both laughed as Connor once again marveled at how wonderful it was to have his sister back. He tried not to dwell too much on all the lost years.

If he thought about it for too long it always took him to a place of resentment and anger.

As everyone joined in to help clean up, Connor began to second-guess his offer to drop off Ella's items at her house. Clearly he'd jumped at the opportunity just so he could spend more time with her, even if it was only a few moments. But he wanted to figure out why she'd been acting so cold.

Connor looked at his watch. He wanted to get over to Ella's house before it got too late. He'd already agreed to help Braden bring some of the gifts over to the new house he'd just built as a wedding surprise for Piper. Once he had done that, he didn't hesitate to get back on the road.

Connor cranked up the volume on the radio. Somebody was singing a poignant country song about losing the love of his life. He drummed his fingers on the steering wheel to the fast tempo. Maybe he should just turn the truck around and go home. Ella seemed to be a private person who might not embrace the idea of him just showing up at her door. His mind kept flitting back to her shuttered expression and closed off body language. Why had he thought that this was a good idea?

He was failing miserably in staying away from Ella. This was a prime example. Connor was going out of his way to be in her presence when he could have left well enough alone. Despite his conflicted feelings about whether Ella was someone he could trust, he liked her. A lot.

Maybe his suspicions about her were nothing more than his own wild imagination. Perhaps he was just used to knowing everything about everyone in his hometown. It wasn't right to judge her for not being an open book and for appearing frightened. If he made a list of pros versus cons, he was certain the pros would far outweigh the cons.

Or maybe he was simply trying to stuff down his grave reservations. She was beautiful and sweet natured, and he didn't want to run the risk of letting something wonderful slip through his fingers.

Yet nothing had changed to allow him to feel confident that Ella wasn't still harboring secrets that might blow up in his face.

Chapter Eleven

~🍃~

Isabelle let out a sigh as she put on a pair of sweats and a comfy top, then settled in with a book of devotionals. It was the perfect way to unwind after a long day. Earlier she had fixed herself a simple meal of pasta and salad for an easy dinner. The bridal shower had been lovely. It had felt good to meet new people and to celebrate Piper and Braden's upcoming wedding. That's what life was all about, and once she'd stopped feeling mopey about her situation, she'd been able to truly appreciate the scope of what she'd experienced.

Back home her family always celebrated birthdays, weddings, anniversaries and graduations in grand style with Brazilian music and amazing food. She missed those moments so much it left an ache in her soul.

Other than the things she'd learned about Connor, it had been a great day. Despite her best intentions, thoughts of the handsome chocolate heir kept creeping into her thoughts. For a variety of reasons, she didn't want to like him. But she did.

"Focus on something else," she said as she turned a page in her book. She began highlighting passages and reciting words out loud.

A whistling sound began to resonate from outside her bedroom window. She sucked in a sharp breath. Perhaps it was just the wind. The strange noises continued, shattering her sense of peace and security. Every creak and groan made her almost jump out of her skin.

Was someone out there in the darkness? Her pulse began to race. She raised a hand to her throat. Isabelle felt paralyzed with fear. Her mind began to whirl with all the possibilities.

Marshal Kramer had assured her that she would be safe here in Owl Creek. At the moment she wondered if he'd been mistaken. Had danger followed her to Alaska?

She needed to stay calm. *When thou passest through the waters, I will be with thee.* The passage from Isaiah came to mind, encouraging her not to allow anxiety to outweigh reason. In all likelihood there was some reasonable explanation for the creepy sounds.

Just breathe, she told herself. *You're letting your imagination run wild.*

Another loud sound echoed in the house, a boom from the rear. Then she heard a shuffling noise that almost sounded like someone was walking up the steps. Isabelle's first instinct was to hide. If only her brain could convince her body to move. Her mind flashed back to the terrifying night a man had broken into her apartment and tried to harm her so she couldn't testify in Burke's trial. That very moment had determined her future in the Witness Protection Program. She had been fortunate to make it out of the situation alive. And now, all these months later she was still in the grip of unrelenting terror.

Even though she'd closed the door on her former life and assumed a new identity to protect herself, Isabelle was still in jeopardy.

As Connor drove up to Ella's dimly lit house, he immediately spotted a few lights glowing from inside the home. He wasn't sure if he should ring the bell or not.

"Just go home," he muttered. "Maybe she's made an early night of it."

He was annoyed at himself because he was acting like an uncertain teenager on his first date. Normally, Connor was pretty composed, and he didn't waste time second-guessing himself. He was simply doing a favor for a friend. *Humph!* Who was he kidding? There was absolutely nothing platonic about the way Ella made him feel. She left him breathless.

He couldn't sit in front of her house all night. Connor let out a frustrated sigh before taking off his seat belt and grabbing the items Sage had given him before exiting his truck.

As he strode to the door he wondered if he could just leave it at her doorstep. With snow expected to fall in a few hours, it probably wouldn't be wise. Just as he raised his hand to rap on the door a scream rang out from inside Ella's house. For a moment he wondered if he'd imagined it. Then he heard it again. A loud, panicked scream.

He pounded on the door, calling out to Ella. Connor pushed his shoulder against the doorjamb, hoping he would be able to gain entry. All of a sudden the door gave way and Ella was standing before him. A look of pure terror was etched on her face.

"Connor! I'm so relieved to see you. I heard noises outside. I think someone was outside trying to break into the house."

Connor could clearly see Ella's discomfort. He didn't want to minimize her concerns, but he knew it would be highly unusual for a break-in to happen in Owl Creek. Because his best friend was town sheriff, Connor knew the statistics. It would be as likely as a heat wave in February.

He gently placed his hands on her shoulders. Connor needed her to stay calm and listen to him. "Ella, try not to panic. Stay right here while I look around the perimeter of the house."

She clung to his jacket, slowly nodding her head as she let go of him. Connor headed outside and walked over to his car, fumbling around in the glove compartment for a flashlight. As soon as he located it, he made his way around the outside.

It didn't take him long to spot the large branches that had fallen on a portion of the roof. They were pretty massive. No doubt the sound of them had been terrifying. He made his way back to the front of the house and went inside. Ella was sitting on the living room couch with wide eyes. He sat down next to her.

"It was two large tree branches that fell on the house. The noises you heard were probably the limbs groaning before it happened. Nothing to worry about. And I didn't see any damage to the roof, but you'll be able to get a better look in the morning."

Ella simply stared at him with her

arms wrapped around her middle. Her whole body was trembling.

"I… I thought I was—"

In that moment, Connor saw it all in her eyes. Terror. Someone had wounded this woman. And she was still living in a place of fear. The scars were visible in her actions, even though she tried to hide them. He'd gotten it all wrong. Ella hadn't done anything wrong in the past. She had been terrorized, to the point where she thought someone was coming after her. In Ella's mind the sound of tree limbs had transformed into her worst nightmare. And although he didn't know exactly who or what was scaring her, he knew it was a very real threat in her eyes.

Connor put his arm around her and pulled her against his chest.

"No one is going to hurt you. Not ever. I won't let them. You're safe, Ella." His voice rang out with intensity. A few weeks ago he hadn't even known this woman, but he knew he would do everything in his power to protect her from harm. From this point forward, he considered it his sacred mission.

She let out a sob, then raised her fisted hand to cover her mouth. He could tell she was trying to rein in her emotions. The sight of her tears threatened to do him in.

He reached out and wiped away her tears with his fingers. "You're safe with me."

"Thank you. But it isn't your job to dry my tears. I'm beginning to feel like a wet blanket."

Connor shook his head and chuckled. "Okay. No more corny jokes for you."

"Well, at least I can laugh at myself," she said, chuckling along with him. "I'm so sorry for being such a mess over a few tree limbs. I can't imagine Beulah freaking out over something like this."

"My grandmother is a tough bird, but so are you. There are all kinds of strength in this world. I admire your willingness to pick up stakes and make a new life for yourself in Alaska."

"Thank you, but Beulah's in a league of her own. She's an incredible woman. It's safe to say I want to be like her when I grow up." Ella's voice sounded wistful, and Connor knew she was feeling badly about her reaction to the noises she'd heard. Maybe even a touch embarrassed.

"I think you're pretty amazing, Ella Perez. Not to mention absolutely beautiful. You don't need to be anyone other than yourself."

Ella bowed her head. Her cheeks looked flushed. "You're being really kind."

Connor reached out and lifted her chin up so he could look her in the eyes. "I'm being honest. You're the most stunning woman I've ever laid eyes on. And you have a lot of strengths." He ran his fingers over her lips, tracing the shape of them. "I hope I'm not out of line, but I'd like to kiss you. I've been wanting to since the first time I saw you."

Even though Connor still wanted to know Ella's truths, he couldn't deny the deep yearning to kiss her and give her comfort. Hopefully, over time, she would confide in him. At the moment, he felt reassured enough to move forward.

As he moved closer, their gazes locked. Ella's eyes widened imperceptibly. The flecks in her brown eyes resembled embers. He leaned over and placed his lips on hers. A sweet floral scent filled his nostrils, instantly bringing to mind Alaska's state flower, forget-me-nots. Her lips were soft and inviting. They tasted like cinnamon and sweetness. She kissed him back with equal measure, her lips moving against his with a tenderness that blew him away. He placed his hand on the back of her neck, anchoring her to him as the kiss intensified. In response, Ella placed her hand on his chest. He wondered if she could tell his heart was beating extra fast.

This was the moment he'd been hoping for over the past few weeks. It gave him confirmation that the attraction wasn't one-sided. Ella felt something for him! In all of his life Connor had never experienced a kiss like this one. It was so natural and tender. It felt like coming home, as if they'd known each other all of their lives. Was this the elusive feeling he'd been missing out on all this time?

For a few moments they were lost in the kiss. Time seemed to stand still. For the life of him Connor didn't want it to end. He didn't want to go back to a place where he still had unanswered questions about Ella. This moment felt so perfect since it came from a place of feeling and not reason. All that mattered was this connection between them.

As the kiss ended and they drew apart, Connor swept his palm against her cheek. She looked up at him, her sooty lashes framing her beautiful eyes. He could stay here for hours just looking at her.

"I should head home. You need to get some sleep, Ella."

"I am feeling pretty tuckered out," she admitted. "Now I can sleep soundly and not worry about strange noises from the darkness."

"I've lived here my whole life. I can't remember a single instance when folks had to worry about break-ins. You're safe here."

He watched as her shoulders sagged in relief. Whatever was troubling her, he was happy he'd been able to allay her fears, even though he was still struggling to figure her out. Connor still felt curious about her situation and who was responsible for frightening her, but he sensed that she wasn't going to open up to him. He had a sinking feeling in his gut. No matter how deeply he wished she would confide in him, only Ella could make that decision. And so far she was choosing not to do so.

As they said good-night by the door, Ella reached up and placed a swift kiss on his cheek. "Thank you, Connor. I don't know what I would have done if you hadn't stopped by."

"I'm glad I did. I actually stopped by to bring you the goody bags from the party. I put them on the table in the foyer."

"Thank you," Ella murmured. "That was very sweet of you."

"I'm here for you, Ella. I'm a good listener and I don't judge. I can be a strong shoulder to lean on if you need one."

His gaze didn't waver as he looked at her. One word from Ella and he would head right back into the house and listen to anything and everything she wanted to tell him. All this time Ella had been an enigma, a puzzle he'd been trying to figure out. Even though they had just shared a tender moment, there were still many pieces missing.

Connor felt a stab of disappointment when she bade him good-night without taking him up on his offer. As he walked to his truck and settled in behind the driver's seat, he couldn't deny the confused feelings warring inside of him. The kiss he'd shared with Ella had been exhilarating. But her secrets still stood between them.

He was impatient to finally get some answers about the things she'd been hiding. Until that time, Connor knew he couldn't offer her anything more than friendship.

Isabelle woke up the following morning from a very unsettled slumber. She knew her sense of unease had everything to do with Connor's visit and the kiss they'd shared. It had felt nice in the moment, but her conscience wouldn't allow her to proceed any further. A man like Connor North deserved truth and transparency, neither of which she could give him.

She had every intention of spending a leisurely Sunday doing a few things around the house after she returned from church. In order to subdue her grumbling stomach, Isabelle headed down to the kitchen and made herself a bowl of oatmeal and two pieces of wheat toast with genuine Alaskan blueberry jam. Despite her state of mind, every bite tasted delectable.

Just as she was about to head upstairs for a shower, a knock sounded on her front door. She looked down at her leisure wear—a pair of sweatpants and a matching top, along with a pair of fuzzy socks. She looked somewhat presentable, she guessed. But what if it was Connor? She really didn't want him to see her looking so frumpy.

Oh, well. If it was Connor, he might as well see her in an unfiltered way since they were stuck in the friend zone. With a sigh, she got up from her chair and headed toward the door. Right before she pulled it open, Isabelle let her hair free from a ponytail holder and shook it loose, running her fingers though the strands to tame it. She yanked open the door as her greeting froze on her lips.

"Jonah! What are you doing here?" The question flew out of her mouth. The U.S. Marshal was standing at her doorstep dressed in a pair of dark jeans, a black puffer jacket and a pair of Ray-Ban sunglasses.

"You sounded pretty frantic during our phone call. My boss agreed it was time for me to make a house call."

"I can't believe you came. Come inside," she said, ushering him into the house.

"Thanks. Homer is just a short flight away," Jonah said as he crossed the threshold and entered her house. "It gave me an opportunity to ride in a seaplane. That doesn't happen every day."

"Why don't we go into the kitchen and I'll make us some hot cocoa," she offered. She had dozens of packets, courtesy of North Star Chocolates.

"Sounds good," Jonah said as he trailed after her and settled himself at her farmhouse-style table while she prepared the cups of hot chocolate. "How are you getting acclimated to Owl Creek?"

"I'm getting there," she said. "It's been difficult at times, especially missing my family." Her throat tightened. "But the people here have been pretty wonderful," she added as Connor's face flashed before her eyes.

"And the company you're working for?" Jonah asked as she placed a cup down in front of him and sat down across from him with her own mug of cocoa.

"So far, it's been incredible. I have nothing to say but positive things." She smiled at Jonah. "What's not to love? I'm able to be around chocolate all day and I get lots of samples to take home. I wish I had more self-control," she admitted with a laugh.

Jonah nodded. "Everything sounds like it's falling into place. I thought you might have packed up your suitcases and given your employer a resignation letter." He took a sip of his cocoa and let out a satisfied sound. "You sounded pretty frantic the other day when we spoke. Even after you found out your photo wasn't going online, I got the impression you were still jittery."

"I was," she answered, shuddering as she remembered her anxiety from a few days ago. She had been in such turmoil that she'd honestly considered leaving Owl Creek and asking to be reassigned to another locale. "Thankfully, the CEO decided my picture was only going to be hung up at the factory and the chocolate shop with only a brief mention in the employee newsletter. I have the feeling her grandson might have told her it made me uncomfortable." She let out a ragged sigh. "I may have overreacted. I'm sorry if you wasted a trip."

"It's not a waste, especially if you've decided to stay put here in town. It gets a bit messy when things fall apart so quickly. As you know, relocating isn't easy. Of course it would be your decision, but you would have to start the whole process all over again. That would be very stressful for you."

Isabelle didn't want to go anywhere. She couldn't imagine finding a better relocation spot than where she'd landed. Now that the panic had dissipated, she could see her situation clearly. Staying put was the best move.

"I like it here. It's miles apart from anything I've ever known, but it's growing on me." It was gratifying being able to give Jonah a good report after the anxiety she'd experienced the other day. It served as a reminder that sometimes she needed to breathe before allowing her mind to take her to dark places. She wanted to be in a place where she was living in a state of grace and not fear.

"That's what we like to hear. Keeping you safe is our number one priority, but we also want you to live the best life possible. A life without fear."

That was her goal as well. It made her soul soar to know she was more than just a case number to the marshals assigned to her protection.

"I have a question for you. Has anything changed with the case? I know it's a long shot, but are there any updates?"

Jonah quirked his mouth. "I hate being the bearer of bad news, but it's part of the job description. One of Burke's cronies who was serving as a witness was killed yesterday."

Isabelle let out a gasp and raised her

hand to her throat. "Oh, no! That's awful."

Jonah's expression was somber. "We have no doubt Burke was behind it. His reach extends beyond prison. The witness wasn't under the protection of WITSEC however, since he refused to participate. Burke has appealed the case, which means it would benefit him if you can't testify in any future trial. You're still in jeopardy, Ella. Don't ever forget it."

Isabelle wrapped her hands around her heated mug. Despite the warmth, she felt a shiver run through her. Jonah didn't pull any punches. Her life was still in danger. Another witness had been killed by Burke. She had no doubt he would enjoy tracking down her whereabouts in Owl Creek and doing the same to her.

After Connor's assurances last night, she was beginning to feel secure in this quaint Alaskan town. As if it was her haven from the ugliness of bullets and violence. For the first time since her arrival, Isabelle could envision living out the rest of her days in Owl Creek. She knew instinctively it had a lot to do with her friendship with Connor.

In the cold light of day, she regretted having kissed him, but her feelings were a bit all over the place. Iris had made it clear to her that Connor was an expert at playing the field. Was she just another conquest? On the other hand, the kiss had given her comfort and a sense of security at a time when she'd badly needed it. And it had offered her hope. Maybe she didn't have to be alone for the rest of her days. But Jonah's announcement brought her squarely back to earth.

After an hour or so of chatting, Jonah announced that he needed to get going. Isabelle no longer felt surprised by the covert actions of Marshal Kramer. Although his visit had been short, she deeply appreciated the face-to-face drop-in to tell her about the witness's murder. Isabelle stood by the door and waved as Jonah drove away in a dark sedan. He was gone just as mysteriously as he'd arrived. She couldn't explain it, but she had the feeling this was the last time she would ever see the U.S. Marshal. Today she felt stronger than she had a few days ago. It was a God moment. All this time she'd been praying for strength, and she finally was feeling empowered.

Even though Jonah had delivered some alarming news it hadn't shattered her. She was still standing. She was committed to living her life without constantly looking over her shoulder. Although it was a sobering reality that her life would always be in danger, she was finally coming to terms with it. She now knew she could face fear head-on and come out the other side. She could make a life for herself in Alaska. It might not be like the one she'd left behind, but it could be a good existence nevertheless.

Hope. In order to make this work, didn't she need to have faith in rebuilding her life?

After she closed the door and came inside from the cold, Isabelle went upstairs to get ready for the late morning service. She had so much to be thankful for, and she wanted to worship with the townsfolk in God's house. Would Connor be in attendance? She was a bit nervous to see him again after the tender kiss they'd shared last night. Isabelle prayed things wouldn't be awkward between them. After all, they were both adults, right? Surely they could both see that the kiss had been ill-advised and a result of the nerve-racking situation she'd found herself in.

Nothing had changed between them,

despite the kiss. It didn't matter how deeply she yearned to push past friendship with Connor. It simply wasn't possible.

Chapter Twelve

On Sunday, Connor didn't have much
time to dwell on the situation with Ella.
Running into Ella after church service
had put things into perspective about
his relationship with her. Just because
he wasn't able to pursue a romance with
Ella didn't mean he couldn't be a good
friend and ally. She was a stranger in
an unfamiliar town that was full of interesting places to explore. He'd invited Ella to go sightseeing with him,
offering himself as her Owl Creek tour
guide.

A few hours later he was with Ella,

staring up at a sky full of stars set against a velvety backdrop. He knew she'd been wanting to get a glimpse of the town's legendary owls, so here they were at their final destination after hours of exploring various locations in town.

He was sitting on a snowbank, shoulder to shoulder with Ella. "See that right there?" he asked, pointing up at the inky sky.

Ella let out a gasp. "What is it? I've never spotted anything like it before."

Connor dragged his eyes away from Ella and looked up at the crimson-colored moon. "They call it a super blood wolf moon. It doesn't come around very often, but when it does, it's spectacular."

"It's stunning. I never even knew it existed."

Connor turned toward her. "Stick around, kid. Alaska has a lot of hidden treasures. You just have to be open to it."

Ella nodded her head vigorously. Her enthusiasm was effusive. She almost resembled a wide-eyed kid with her excitement. Her brown eyes shone with wonder.

"It's funny how the things that are truly wonderful always seem to come out of the blue. Like a double rainbow or a shooting star. Or in this case, a super blood wolf moon." Her tinkling laughter filled the air. He wanted to hear more of it. The smiles. The joy. The happiness. It only served to enhance her natural beauty.

"Wait till you see the northern lights. Every time I witness them, it makes me feel like a kid on Christmas morning," Connor said.

"Well then, I hope to catch a glimpse one of these days."

"Oh, you'll need more than a peek. Hopefully it won't just be a flash. The best sightings are the ones that stick around for a while."

They sat for a few moments in companionable silence. It was nice that neither one of them needed to fill up the silence. He could sit like this for hours just gazing up at the heavens. Even the frigid temperatures weren't a problem right now. All was right in his world.

"Look. It's a snowy owl!" she cried out, pointing at the bird gracefully flying through the air. "It's so beautiful."

"Alaska is really showing off for you tonight. A blood moon and a snowy owl. You're really getting a show."

She shook her head, her long strands of hair whirling around her shoulders. "I'm glad you brought me here tonight. It's perfect."

As their eyes met, something shimmered and pulsed in the air between them. He reached out and clasped her hand in his, pulling her closer. What he saw glistening in her eyes reflected his own sentiments.

"Ella," he murmured, dipping his head

down toward her. Her eyes fluttered closed, and he knew she anticipated the kiss as he made his move. He pressed his lips against Ella's. He thought he heard her let out a little sigh of appreciation. He took her face in his hands and tenderly moved his lips over hers. She wrapped her arms around his neck and pulled him closer.

He'd never been one to talk about romantic moments, but this tender interlude was everything. Their first kiss had been a sweet exploration, whereas this one was filled with more emotion. He could feel her heart fluttering inside her chest. It matched the beats of his own. He thought it might burst straight out of his chest. Feeling these emotions was confusing, since he was determined to avoid any romantic entanglements with Ella. At the moment he knew he was playing with fire.

If it was at all possible, Connor would stay here with Ella until the diamond-like stars were erased from the sky. He cared about this woman way more than he wanted to. She'd managed to burrow her way into his heart when he wasn't looking. And now all he wanted in this world was to be with her. Every second they shared was sacred to him because, as much as he wished a future with her was possible, it wasn't when he still couldn't be sure of what she was hiding.

Connor still wondered what she was running from. What could possibly be so awful that she was determined to keep it under wraps? He winced as his mind began whirling with awful possibilities. Try as he might, Connor couldn't stop thinking about the terrible price his own family had paid at the hands of a woman who'd harbored devastating secrets. Jane Duncan had stolen his sister due to the fact that she'd been unable to have her own child. It was only on her deathbed that she'd confessed her sins to Sage. His family had never received a word of apology from her for her heinous act. Her actions had wounded all of them in the worst possible way.

There was no way in this world he could allow it to happen to his family again.

Over the next few weeks, Ella became more entrenched in the vital community of Owl Creek. Joining the choir, making new friends at North Star Chocolates and spending time with Connor helped make her feel as if the small Alaskan town was becoming a home. While it had once been a hideaway, a safe place to live while she was rebuilding her life, now it was so much more. It was a place where she could imagine herself growing old. She was sure of that this morning when she had received an invitation to Piper and Braden's wedding. She couldn't stop gazing at the beautiful stationery and thinking how fortunate she was to be invited to the nuptials. Getting the special piece of mail made her grin from ear to ear.

When she gazed at the invitation for the hundredth time she found herself tracing the gold script that spelled out Ella Perez. Tears sprang to her eyes. Would she ever get used to this? Being someone other than her truest self? Sometimes she wanted to scream out that she was Isabelle Sanchez from Miami, Florida. But she couldn't. Not if she wanted to stay out of Vincent Burke's reach.

Ella Perez wasn't real. Her story was a fabrication. Her own life had been erased. She needed to accept it.

Isabelle couldn't get any closer to Connor with all these secrets lurking under the surface. What if one of Burke's men did come looking for her in Alaska? Connor might be placed in jeopardy simply by his connection to her. She couldn't let that happen.

She still had nightmares from time to time, but they were less frequent than they had been when she'd first arrived in town. Isabelle had taken some steps forward over the last few weeks—she no longer jumped at sudden noises or had flashbacks of the shooting. For the first time in a long time she didn't have a tight sensation across her chest. She could breathe now.

The biggest thing weighing her down was the knowledge that she couldn't tell Connor a single thing about her past. Sometimes she had the impression he suspected something. He would look at her strangely at random moments or ask probing questions. Perhaps she was just feeling funny about living a life that really wasn't her own. Maybe she was projecting her worries onto him. Even if they could never be a couple, he'd proven himself to be a solid friend.

"You're Ella Perez now," she said out loud as she gazed into the mirror. Although she looked the same as she always had, Isabelle knew she was changing every single day. Pretty soon, Isabelle would be nothing more than a memory.

And it broke her heart into a million little pieces.

Connor parked his truck a block away from the Snowy Owl Diner and began walking down Main Street. He was in the mood for a little walk down the main thoroughfare. He forced himself to smile at the townsfolk he crossed paths with, engaging in light conversation before going on his way. It was a gorgeous February morning with freshly fallen snow glistening on the tree branches. Everyone seemed to be out and about, frequenting the shops, running errands or indulging in an aromatic cup of tea at Tea Time. Normally, he would feel upbeat on a day like this, but Connor's mood was contemplative. He'd arisen this morning with more questions than answers. He didn't enjoy feeling so unsettled. Was he making too much of an issue about Ella's mysterious past? It was still weighing on him.

He didn't have to know everything about Ella's history in order to know he was falling in love with the beautiful newcomer. Maybe that's what he should focus on. The hope that one day they could turn their friendship into something more.

"Morning, Trudy," he said as he spotted the lovable innkeeper.

Trudy Miller greeted him warmly. "Hey there, Connor. Nice to see you. I think your two sidekicks are waiting for you at the diner."

"I'm on my way," he said, pausing to plant a kiss on her cheek as he breezed by.

Trudy grinned and waved him down the street.

A few steps later he almost collided with Maya Roberts, the town's veterinarian.

"Woops. Sorry, Maya. I wasn't paying attention," he apologized.

Maya smiled. "No worries. I just sent you a postcard. It's time Bear came in for his shots."

"Thanks for the reminder. I'll bring him in ASAP," he said before continuing on toward the diner. Things had been so hectic lately. He'd completely forgotten about Bear's annual shots.

Connor bounded up the diner stairs and held the door open as his friend, Otis Cummings, exited the establishment with his lady friend, Birdie McCuller. Otis frequented the diner for breakfast several times a week. The older man was dipping his toe into the relationship pool after losing his wife a year ago. It was nice to see Otis so happy with Birdie.

"Hey there, Connor," Otis said, tipping his hat at him.

"You're such a sweetheart," Birdie crowed as she sailed through the door. "And a true blue gentleman."

"Have a great day, you two," Connor said as he stepped inside. The smell of pancakes and eggs hovered in the air, causing his stomach to grumble in appreciation. He'd woken up to a hearty appetite and he was eager to dig in to one of the diner's breakfast specials.

He spotted Gabe and Hank at their usual table at the back of the restaurant. As soon as he sat down in the booth, his friends greeted him.

"Well, look who's gracing us with his presence," Hank drawled. "A sight for sore eyes."

"I barely recognize him," Gabe said, giving Connor the once-over.

"Give it a rest, guys. It hasn't been that long." Connor forced himself to smile. The last thing he needed was for his two best friends to pounce on him. They were both pretty intuitive about Connor's state of mind. He knew it was only a matter of time before one of them brought up Ella.

Rosie, one of the new waitresses, brought over a carafe of orange juice and began filling their glasses before taking their orders.

"So where've you been?" Hank inquired once Rosie left. "Rumor has it you've been seen around town with a certain dark-haired beauty."

"Yeah. We've been spending time together. Just as friends, though. It's not exactly front-page news," Connor said. He wasn't at all surprised that his name had been linked with Ella's. Connor felt a stab of disappointment that the townsfolk had gotten it all wrong. His relationship with Ella had never developed into a romantic one. He was partly to blame for it, due to his overly suspicious nature.

Gabe chuckled. "You clearly don't know the people in this town. They live for this kind of stuff. Next thing you know they'll be marrying the two of you off."

Connor rolled his eyes. He loved how people went from zero to a hundred in the span of a few weeks. He hoped Ella didn't catch wind of any of the rumors. Connor knew Ella didn't want a romantic relationship. He would hate for her to feel any awkwardness about being the focus of town gossip.

Connor needed to make sure his best friends understood. "She's pretty amazing, although we're just friends."

"Are you sure? That look on your face suggests otherwise," Gabe remarked.

He shook his head. "Yeah, I am. We were getting close, but honestly, I have so many doubts about her past. So we're just buddies."

Hank leaned across the table. "Are

you saying you'd like to be more than friends in the future?"

Connor quirked his mouth. "I'd like to, but it's not possible. She's not interested in me that way."

"It's nice she had a visitor," Gabe said, taking a huge sip of his juice. "It's never easy starting over in a new town."

Connor frowned. "A visitor? No, you've got it wrong. I don't think any of her family or friends have come to see her. She's been talking a lot about being homesick."

Gabe scoffed. "Well, someone did. A man chartered a flight a few weeks ago. Lawson Charters had to communicate with his plane to make sure we weren't in the same airspace. The plane landed at my hangar."

His throat felt dry. Owl Creek was only accessible via plane and water. Coming to town wasn't an easy process. Surely Gabe wouldn't have gotten it wrong. Suddenly, Connor's stomach was tied up in knots. This felt off. Why hadn't Ella mentioned having a visitor, especially since she'd confided in him about yearning for her loved ones?

Rosie returned with their orders, but all of a sudden he wasn't hungry. He knew that he wouldn't even be able to swallow. Connor couldn't shake off the feeling that once again Ella was hiding something.

"How do you know he was here to see Ella?" he asked Gabe.

Gabe locked gazes with him. "You know how small towns are. Nothing's invisible. One of my mechanics spotted him coming and going from Ella's house. And he said this wasn't his first visit."

Town gossips! He clenched his jaw as heat spread through his chest. Didn't people in Owl Creek have anything better to do than flap their jaws? Resentment flooded him. He didn't even know why he was getting so wound up over it, but he felt aggravated.

"I wish people would mind their business." Connor angrily spit out the words.

"What are you getting so upset about?" Hank asked. His face was creased with a frown.

"I'm not upset," Connor said, denying the raw emotions he was battling.

"I shouldn't have said anything," Gabe muttered. "Next time I'm going to mind my business."

"You don't have to treat me with kid gloves, Gabe," he snapped.

"If that's the case, I'm just going to ask… What's bugging you?" Gabe asked. "From what you've said, you and Ella are just friends."

"We are, but I can't pretend I don't wish something deeper has been brewing between us," Connor said.

"Don't be that guy, okay? Just because she had a man visit her, you can't assume it was romantic," Gabe said. "Don't let a misunderstanding get in the way of something terrific."

Although he was experiencing a little spurt of jealousy, that wasn't the main issue. The bigger question was why hadn't Ella told him a friend was flying into Owl Creek. Why were there so many things about her past she seemed to be hiding? Just who was Ella Perez? Gabe's mention of the mysterious visitor to Owl Creek was the final straw. He'd allowed his feelings for Ella to cloud his judgment. He had suspected something was off with her since the very beginning.

"It's not just that," he said, letting out a deep sigh. "There's a dozen reasons why I couldn't allow myself to get involved with Ella. I would've had to push past every single doubt I had and allowed my heart to rule my head. And trust me, there have been times when I wanted to do just that."

"We thought you'd put those issues to rest," Hank said. "I guess we assumed since the two of you were spending a lot of time together that you trusted her. Even in a friendship that's important."

"To be honest, the doubts never went away. Maybe I was just fooling myself, thinking it wasn't necessary to have full disclosure in a friendship. I can't explain how overwhelming it is. It feels like a tidal wave is crashing over me." He ran a shaky hand over his face.

"Talk to her," Gabe said. "Tell her how you feel. Straighten things out before it festers, Connor."

"I second that," Hank added. "If you want to squash these reservations, put it all out there. Don't leave anything unsaid. If she's as special as you believe, she'll have answers for you."

Connor nodded. "Thanks. That's exactly what I intend to do. And there's no time like the present." He gritted his teeth. "I need answers. And I need them now."

Chapter Thirteen

Despite Gabe's and Hank's attempts to settle his nerves, Connor hadn't been able to calm down. He hadn't been able to eat his breakfast and he'd bolted from the diner as soon as the tab was paid. He didn't even bother calling Ella before showing up at her house. They'd talked last night, and she'd told him she was going to be running some errands, but Connor was just going to take a chance she'd be there. When he pulled up, he spotted her truck outside the house, serving as confirmation that she was inside.

Finding out about her mysterious guest had caused something inside of him to crack wide-open. For the entire time Ella had been in Owl Creek, Connor had questioned her truthfulness. Now it felt like she'd smacked him straight in the face with her evasions.

Was he blowing things out of proportion? He didn't want to barge into her house spewing accusations. His fervent hope was that she would have a simple answer to his question that would quell all of his uncertainties.

Lord, please give me clarity. I'm so confused right now, and I don't want to let anger cloud my objective. I need answers from Ella. I want the truth. Please grant me the strength to deal with whatever she might tell me.

When he knocked on the door, Ella answered it with a look of surprise mixed with joy etched on her face. "Connor! I wasn't expecting you. Come on in," she said. Ella was treating him like a treasured guest, and it gutted him.

This wasn't a friendly visit. He'd come here seeking answers, and he wasn't going to allow her to deflect or steer him away from his purpose.

"Can I get you anything? I made some biscuits earlier and—"

"No," he said quickly, cutting her off. He needed to talk to her before he lost his nerve. There was something about Ella that always made him feel badly about questioning her. "I've already had breakfast at the diner. I need to talk to you about something."

"All right," she said. "Why don't we go to the living room and sit down?"

Connor trailed after her, all the while thinking of what he wanted to say. When Ella sat down on the couch, he resisted the urge to sit next to her. Instead he sat in a high-backed chair across from her.

"Is everything okay? You seem upset."

He inhaled a calming breath. "I heard something earlier from Gabe. He said you had a visitor fly in from out of town. Is that true?" He was watching her reaction carefully, eager to see her response.

Ella looked like a deer caught in the headlights. She was staring at him with big eyes and picking idly at her long-sleeved shirt. "Yes, it's true," she said in a halting voice.

"Who is he?"

"H-he's a friend."

His jaw clenched. So why hadn't she told him? Why had it been such a secret?

He knitted his brows together. "From where? What's his name?"

"Connor, what's going on? Why are you grilling me like this?" She wiped her hand across her forehead. She appeared to be nervous. In his heart he'd wanted her to be calm, cool and collected with nothing kept secret.

His heart sank. She was getting defensive and not giving him any of the answers he so desperately needed. Perhaps he was springing this on her, but if she wasn't keeping him in the dark it shouldn't be a problem. And it wasn't just this omission. There had been so many piling up for weeks now. He cared so very deeply about her. Getting to the truth was the only way they might ever have a chance at a future together. And if he was being honest with himself, that's what he wanted more than anything.

"Has he been here before?" he asked, his suspicions intensifying with every passing second.

Ella bit her lip. She nodded. "Yes. Once before. When I first came to Owl Creek he helped me get settled."

A feeling of disbelief swept through him. Clearly this man was important to her. He wasn't a member of her family, and yet she wasn't doing much explaining about his presence in her life. If he didn't suspect she was sitting on a world of secrets, maybe this development wouldn't bother him so much. In many ways it was the final straw of weeks spent wondering about the skeletons in Ella's closet. He'd had enough!

"His name is Jonah. Like I said, he's a friend."

"He flew all the way here, but you didn't want to introduce him to anyone? Show him around town?" If Ella had toured a stranger around town, Connor would have heard about it. The town gossips would have had a field day over it. But at least it would have been done out in the open. It would make sense.

She looked down instead of meeting his gaze. "H-he wasn't here long. There really wasn't time for sightseeing."

Connor shook his head. It made no sense. Ella was playing him for a fool and pretending as if her actions weren't suspicious. It felt like she was gaslighting him.

"You said you're not used to snow, but Flagstaff gets tons of it," he blurted out. "You didn't know how to drive in the snow. You were completely unnerved when I wanted to take your ID picture. You didn't want your picture put online. And the very first day we met you didn't answer me when I called out your name. How do you explain these inconsistencies?"

"I... I can't explain those things, Connor." Her tone was flat and unemotional.

"Can't or won't?" he asked. Frustration had gotten the better of him. Although he felt badly about blindsiding her with his questions, he'd been driven to the brink. He was trying to bridge this chasm between them, but she wasn't giving him anything to hold on to. She wasn't giving him any answers. Nothing made sense. At this point he wasn't even sure he could justify a friendship with her based on all of her evasions. After what his family had experienced in the past, Connor knew better than to ignore warning signs.

Ella wasn't even trying to make eye contact with him now. She was shutting down on him, and he had no idea of how to get through to her. Perhaps he was being too insensitive. Maybe she needed a sympathetic approach.

He softened his voice. "Ella, I know you might be scared. I think you've been through something that frightened you. I think there are things you haven't been able to express."

Ella's expression was shuttered. How could she be this calm? She wasn't reacting as if any of this was a big deal at all. Didn't she care about how he felt?

"Ella, I grew up with secrets. My whole childhood was affected by lies and deception. I can't go through that again. It hurt too much the first time.

And that pain only recently began to heal with Sage's return. I care about you, but I can't be involved with someone who won't be honest with me. The truth is too important to hide."

"I understand," she said calmly.

"Is there anything you'd like to tell me?" he asked, offering her a final chance to open up to him. "I'm here, Ella. Here beside you, willing to listen."

For a moment he thought he'd gotten through to her. She met his gaze and he saw a spark of something in her eyes that made him believe she cared about him enough to unveil herself.

"No, Connor. There isn't," she answered.

Her response almost brought him to his knees. He'd been holding on to hope until this very moment and praying for her to come to her senses. Instead, she'd flatly rejected his plea. And judging by the reserved look on her face, it didn't bother her at all.

He let out a ragged sigh, then stood up from his seat. "Thanks, Ella. You've made everything perfectly clear. I'll see myself out."

Just as he reached the door, Ella called out to him. "Connor. Wait!"

Hope rocketed inside of him. *Please, God. Answer my prayer.*

"I'm so sorry," she said.

"I am, too," Connor said before stepping out the door. He didn't bother looking back. Ella had made it clear that she wasn't willing to bend in order to be with him.

After he got in his truck, Connor roared down the road, trying his best to leave all thoughts of Ella Perez in his rearview mirror.

As she covertly peered through the window and watched Connor drive away, Isabelle's heart cracked into a million pieces. She knew she should feel relieved that her friendship with

Connor was over. At least now she wouldn't have to feel guilty any longer about the secrets she was withholding from him. She wouldn't have to agonize about every slip of the tongue or the answers she could never provide to his questions. Shouldn't she feel free right now? Free from having to tell the man she loved more lies. Somewhere along the way she'd fallen in love with Connor, which totally explained the knife-like sensation twisting in her gut. He would no longer be involved in her life. She'd seen it written all over his face right before he left.

When she was a little girl, she'd had a habit of curling up into a little ball and shutting out the world anytime she had been in pain. Although she'd outgrown the habit, this fresh hurt made her long to revert back to old patterns. Maybe she could forget about Connor and her feelings for him. Perhaps it wouldn't hurt so badly if she stuffed them all down into a vast black hole and pretended as if nothing had happened between them at all.

When thou walkest through the fire, thou shalt not be burned; neither shall the flame kindle upon thee.

Yet she did feel terribly burned. She had gotten way too close to Connor, mistakenly believing that friendship would suffice even though her feelings had blossomed over time. Isabelle had hurt him. She'd seen the raw pain emanating from his eyes. He was a proud man who always tried to shield himself from emotional upheaval. It was a defense mechanism he'd constructed as a child due to the trauma of Sage's abduction. And now, thanks to her, Connor was dealing with more anguish. She'd wounded him. And that knowledge caused a twisting sensation in the pit of her stomach. Tears swept down her face. She'd lost Connor's goodwill and friendship. Their relationship had been littered with half-truths. The foundation had been weak at its core.

He didn't even know her real name. She'd never had the pleasure of hearing him call her Isabelle. And now she never would. Everything felt bleak now. Suddenly her life in Owl Creek felt smaller and less substantial. Connor's absence would leave a hole the size of Kachemak Bay.

Lord, please help me heal this broken heart. I love this man with all of my soul and I can't erase what he means to me. The emotions run too deep. He's too firmly embedded in my heart. And I fear he will always be there.

A knock on her door startled her from her prayers. Was it Connor? Had he come back to try to straighten things out? She raced to the door and flung it open, wanting nothing more than to see Connor's handsome face greeting her. Her body sagged as she saw Sage standing at her doorstep.

"Sage," she said. Isabelle could hear the disappointment lacing her own voice.

"Ella! Did you forget I was swinging by to pick you up?" Sage asked.

"Yes. No. I guess so," she said. She'd made plans with Sage to check out the vintage store on Main Street. They were meeting up with Piper and Rachel so they could shop and have lunch together at the diner.

"What's wrong? You look shattered. Did something happen?"

"Oh, no. I'm fine," she said. Her voice was trembling and she could feel the hot sting of tears in her eyes. Before she knew it, tears were streaming down her face.

Sage reached out and pulled her into her arms. Something broke inside her as Sage began whispering soothing words of encouragement. Isabelle began to sob, huge heart-wrenching cries spilling out of her. She had been trying to hold it together for so long now. In the process she had stuffed down all of her feelings of distress, anxiety and pain. In order to make a successful transition to the Witness Protection Program, Isabelle had been forced to maintain a good-natured facade so as not to arouse suspicion. It had all taken a tremendous toll on her.

She wasn't fine. Not by a long shot.

Connor wasn't all right. The weight of pretending as if everything was fine was beginning to weigh on him. He'd managed to sit through a special dinner at his parents' house without choking on his food. Thankfully, the dinner was in Piper and Braden's honor. All attention was focused on their wedding tomorrow. Just watching the joyous couple made him think about Ella and all that she meant to him. It hurt so much to come to terms with the fact that she didn't trust him enough to come clean. Why did this cause him so much angst? Why did she have such an effect on him?

Needing a breath of fresh air, Connor walked toward the front door, shrugging into his jacket before heading outside. The moon hung up in the velvety darkness like a beacon guiding travelers home. He thought back to the night he'd watched the blood moon with Ella and they'd shared tender kisses. That evening had been full of so much promise. Until the bottom had fallen out of his world.

How could he heal this awful ache inside of him when he couldn't even look at an Alaskan sky without thinking about her? Missing her. Wanting to hold her in his arms. Wanting way more than he'd ever been able to claim.

A slight sound caused him to turn around. His grandfather was behind him, bundled up in his winter coat.

"What're you doing out here? It's pretty cold this evening."

"I just needed to be alone with my thoughts," Connor said. "No offense."

"None taken. You've been awfully quiet lately. That's not like you," the older man observed.

"I'm just tired. I've been working too hard, I suppose." He winked at his grandfather. "You need to tell that wife of yours to go easy on me."

Jennings chuckled. "As if she'd listen."

"I need to get some sleep before the wedding tomorrow. It's going to be a big day for our family." What he wasn't saying was that sleep had been elusive lately. More times than not, he tossed and turned until the wee hours of the morning. All was not right within his soul.

"A joyful event. It's just what we need after so many years of sorrow."

For a moment they both settled into

the silence. After all they had endured during the years when Sage was missing, a wedding truly was a blessed event.

Weeping may endure for a day, but joy cometh in the morning. The passage from Psalms resonated with him. It always reminded him of his family and what they'd been through. It was finally their time to experience unbridled joy.

"So, if you don't mind my asking, what's going on with you and Ella? I thought the two of you were on track to become Owl Creek's next sweethearts."

Connor made a face. "It never got off the ground. We were just too different, I suppose." He didn't want to tell his grandfather the nitty-gritty details that had prevented him from getting romantically involved with her.

"That's a shame. She's a fascinating woman."

Connor turned toward his grandfather. "What do you mean? You barely know her."

His grandfather chuckled. "I'm not just a bird-watcher, son. I'm a people watcher, too. I've only been in Ella's presence a few times, but I came to the conclusion that she's not as she appears to be."

Connor let out a brittle laugh. "You're way smarter than I am. It took me months to confirm it."

Jennings narrowed his gaze as he looked at him. "And what exactly did you deduce about Ella?"

"That she's not a truthful person. I have no use for people I can't trust." He hated speaking badly about Ella, but he needed to be honest with his grandfather.

"Hmm. That's not what I observed."

"Don't leave me hanging. I'd love to know your thoughts," Connor said, folding his arms across his chest.

"I saw the pain beneath her beautiful exterior, along with a trace of fear. She tried to hide those things, but I recognized them. When I first met your grandmother, she radiated those same emotions. But, with time and patience, I broke through her tough exterior and found a sparkling diamond underneath."

Connor couldn't imagine two people being more different. His grandmother was as tough as an Alaskan winter on the tundra, while Ella reminded him of forget-me-nots—beautiful yet delicate. He didn't quite see the resemblance.

"Why was grandmother in pain?" he asked.

"People come to us as they are. Beulah's childhood was miserable. It's one of the reasons she was so happy to join the North fold. She didn't just emerge from the womb as the magnificent woman she is today. She grew and evolved over time. Imagine if I'd written her off back then?" Jennings had a contemplative expression on his face.

"I would have missed out on so many wonderful moments."

"You wouldn't have lived out your amazing love story," Connor said. "And I wouldn't be here right now."

Jennings nodded his head. "Amen. Connor, I'd like to ask you a question. Do you love her?"

The question was thrown at him like a curveball. All this time he'd been Ella's friend. They'd never really moved past that stage. Did he love her? He'd never been in love before. Hadn't even come close. He froze for a moment, overwhelmed by the reality of his situation. All of these emotions roiling around inside him added up to one thing. The realization hit him squarely in the chest. He was head over heels in love with Ella.

"Yes, I do. I love her more than I ever imagined I could love someone," he confessed. Something told him that his grandfather already knew what he'd just admitted. He didn't look at all surprised by Connor's declaration.

"So what are you going to do about it?"

"What can I do? Loving her doesn't negate the fact that she won't open up to me about her past. How can I move forward without complete honesty? Not to mention I have no idea if she loves me."

"You have to ask yourself what's worse. Living a life with unanswered questions or living a life without the woman that you love. And if you truly love her, you need to start putting the pieces together. Why would she have come to a remote Alaskan town? Why is she so skittish? Add up everything you know about her. Fill in the blanks. Do some digging on your own."

The words crashed over him with the force of a tsunami. They were powerful and heart-wrenching and moving. And it caused his brain to go into overdrive.

His grandfather put his arm around

him. "Let's go inside. Get some rest. You have a lot of thinking to do."

He did. And even though he needed to get plenty of rest in preparation for Braden's wedding festivities, something told him he wasn't going to sleep a wink tonight. He was going to do a deep dive on the internet, checking in places like Arizona and Florida to see if he could unearth anything about any criminal cases. Perhaps she'd been a victim of an assault or a stalking. If there was even a shred of information, Connor was determined to find it.

Isabelle sat in her truck and looked out her window at the festively decorated church. Flowers had been artfully placed by the entrance along with pink ribbons and an elaborate wedding banner. She watched as guests streamed into the church. Most of them she recognized from around town.

Isabelle had thought about not attending the wedding, but after realizing it wouldn't be right not to show up, she'd decided to honor her commitment. She looked in the rearview mirror, checking to make sure her hair and lipstick were in order. She knew there was a chance she might run into Connor. Her stomach was full of butterflies about how she should react to seeing him, especially now that she knew she was in love with him. Should she casually say hello or avoid him at all costs? It would be for the best if their paths didn't cross. It would be easier for both of them.

A quick glance at her watch served as a warning to go inside the church before Piper made her grand entrance. Once inside, she made a point to sit toward the rear. She didn't want to draw any attention to herself. She'd already had a few townsfolk question her about the rumors about her and Connor over the past week. It had been very awkward and uncomfortable. Somehow she'd managed to answer them tactfully.

From her vantage point she was able to see Connor standing right next to Braden at the altar. Even at this distance he caused a riot of emotions within her. Most of all, a yearning to be with him tugged at her. If only the situation was different.

When the wedding march played, three adorable toddlers teetered down the aisle—a pair of brown-skinned twins, Faith and Lizzie, who she knew belonged to Rachel and Gabe, along with Addie, Hank and Sage's little girl. The little ones practically stole the show until Piper appeared with Hank at her side. Connor had told her that Piper's dad, Jack, had died four years ago in a snowmobile accident. Isabelle imagined having her brother standing in as a substitute was an emotional moment. Tears pooled in Ella's eyes as she watched Piper, resplendent in a white lace and tulle long-sleeved dress, glide by. There was nothing but pure joy etched on her lovely face. She looked like a fairy-tale princess.

Isabelle dabbed at her eyes throughout the awe-inspiring ceremony. Their vows were achingly romantic. When Piper and Braden were declared man and wife, they joined hands and walked back down the aisle followed by their bridal party. As Isabelle spotted Connor approaching, she braced herself for him to look away from her, but as he passed by, their eyes met. The way he stared at her caused her pulse to quicken. Instead of anger, Isabelle saw tenderness.

Stop being fanciful, she urged herself. If nothing else, Connor had made his feelings quite clear to her. He didn't think she was a good person. That realization still hurt.

Isabelle waited till the church was almost empty before she exited. Given the circumstances, she didn't think she would go to the reception at the North estate. It wouldn't feel right since she and Connor were at odds. He should be able to enjoy his brother's special day without any distractions. That's what she was at this point.

When she pushed open the door and walked into the vestibule area, Isabelle sucked in a shocked breath. Connor was standing a few feet away with an earnest expression on his face. It was just the two of them in the corridor. Her first instinct was to retreat, but if the last few months had taught her anything at all, it was to tap into her inner strength. *Fear thou not; for I am with thee.* She wasn't standing alone. He was always with her.

"Ella. It's good to see you." His deep, soothing voice was music to her ears.

Her stomach lurched. Why did he have to look so handsome in his dark suit and tie? Had his eyes always been so blue? It was true what they said. Absence made the heart grow fonder. Isabelle knew down to the days and hours how long it had been since they'd spoken to each other. She ached from missing him.

"Hey, Connor. How are you?" Isabelle forced the words out of her mouth. She was desperate to appear as if her heart hadn't been crushed.

"I'd like to talk to you, if it's all right?" he asked.

"Don't you need to go to the reception?" Isabelle knew the bridal party and the family usually departed together. No doubt they would be looking for Connor outside.

"It can wait. I told them to go on without me."

Isabelle nodded. "Okay," she said, her mind whirling with questions. What could he possibly want to talk to her about? Hadn't they already said it all? Her heart began to thunder wildly inside her chest. Was she being fired from

North Star Chocolates? That would be a devastating blow.

She raised a hand to her throat. "Are you letting me go from the chocolate shop?" she asked. What would she do for work now in Owl Creek? Did this mean she would be forced to relocate?

"Of course not," he said. "Why would you ever think that?"

She let out a sigh of relief. "I... I really love working there and I just thought—"

"I'm sorry, Ella," he said, cutting her off. "I've been doing a lot of thinking. About you. About the things I know you're keeping under wraps. The fear. Your inability to open up to me. The sketchy details about your life. I kept going back to that day in the chocolate shop when the car backfired. You were terrified. Now that I think about it, you were exhibiting signs of post-traumatic stress." He took a deep breath. "I think you witnessed an act of violence. I think you're here because you're a witness.

A few years ago Hank told Gabe and me about a program where witnesses to violent crimes are placed under protection and given a new identity." His voice suddenly sounded hoarse. "I think that's you, Ella."

She let out a sob, then covered her mouth with her hand. Shock roared through her. Connor continued talking.

"I did some fishing around on the internet last night. At first I was searching Arizona cases, but then I looked in Florida since you mentioned spending time there. That's when I found it. You provided testimony after witnessing your boss's murder. Because of you, he was put away for a long time. But it didn't stop his criminal enterprise from coming after you. Which, I suspect, is why you might have entered WITSEC. To save your life." He pulled a piece of paper from his pocket and unfolded it before holding it out to her. "This is you, isn't it? Isabelle Sanchez from Miami, Florida."

Isabelle looked at the printout of the newspaper article. It was all there in black and white. She wiped away tears with the back of her hand. The rules of the WITSEC program didn't stipulate what to do if the person you were madly in love with came to you with decisive proof about your former identity. He was holding the evidence in his hands. She'd done her very best to protect herself and to uphold the standards of the program. But this was an extraordinary development in her story.

Her heart began to thunder in her chest. Because Connor had stumbled upon the truth, her status in WITSEC could be compromised. She might be relocated from Owl Creek to another location. She might have to say goodbye to Connor. The very thought of it caused a twisting sensation in her gut. Words were stuck in her throat.

"I'm sorry for not being gentler with you. I let my pride and my past get the better of me. I'm ashamed of how I acted. I'm asking you to forgive me, but I understand if you can't." He reached out and took her hand. "I want to move forward with you. I know your life is complicated and fraught with danger, but I'm prepared to never divulge a word of this to a single person."

"What are you saying, Connor?" She was practically holding her breath waiting for him to spell it out. Hope was within her grasp and she wanted so badly to grab ahold of it. If there was any chance that they could work through her being in WITSEC, she wouldn't hesitate to do whatever she could to make it happen. She believed in Connor. He would be worth it.

"I thought that I needed to know everything about you in order to forge a relationship with you, but I already know all the things that matter or will ever matter. I know how it makes me feel when you smile at me. I know you would never hurt anyone. You radiate kindness and empathy. I know someone hurt you and made you fearful. And that makes me angrier than I can ever express in words, but I also know it's made you strong and resilient." He took a deep, steadying breath. "I don't want to spend another day apart from you. My life is richer with you in it. I've been so consumed with your past I forgot to focus on the present and the future. Our future. For so long there was a big hole inside me that needed to be filled up. You've done that, Ella. And I don't want to live a life without you in it."

Tears were streaming down her face. She let out a sob. "Are you sure? My life is a bit complicated, and there are lots of dos and don'ts involved. And there's no guarantee that danger might not present itself, not only for myself, but to you as well. And the Marshals might decide to relocate me to another town. That's a distinct possibility now."

"Ella, I'm more certain about us than I've been of anything in my life." Connor reached out and ran his thumb against her cheek. "I love you."

"I love you, too, Connor. So very much," she whispered.

She stood on her tippy-toes and placed a kiss on his lips. In this one moment she was happier than she'd ever imagined. Connor loved her! He'd put the pieces together, and she didn't have to worry about hiding the truth from him because he already knew it. She'd have to convince Jonah that she be allowed to stay now that Connor knew about her past. There were still obstacles to face. But for now she wanted to revel in this moment.

"There's one thing I'd like you to do," she said as their embrace ended.

"Anything."

"Now that you know my real name,

please call me Isabelle just this once." She grinned up at him, buoyed by the love she saw radiating from his eyes. Her emotions threatened to burst out of her chest. She was deliriously happy.

"Isabelle," he murmured. "I like the sound of that."

Hearing her real name rolling off his lips was such a simple thing, yet it filled her with unimaginable bliss.

Epilogue

A light snow gently fell from the sky as Isabelle and Connor burst through the wooden doors of the church followed by a crowd of well-wishers. Happiness hung in the air as the newly married couple was bombarded with forget-me-not flower petals and shouts of congratulations.

Connor reached for his wife's hand and pressed it to his lips. "I love you, Mrs. North."

She was no longer keeping any secrets from her husband. Jonah had met with her and Connor. He'd given her the green light to discuss her participation in WITSEC with Connor since he'd already uncovered the truth online. Connor had reassured Jonah that he would never divulge Isabelle's secrets or put her in harm's way. Thankfully, the marshal hadn't found it necessary to relocate her from Owl Creek. Everything had come full circle for them. Truths had been brought out into the light. Joy shone brightly in the aftermath.

"And I love you, my husband." Tears of contentment pooled in her eyes. She'd never dared to dream of such a wonderful happy ending for herself and Connor. It had seemed so out of reach until Connor put his faith in their relationship before his doubts. His belief in her and their love had been a powerful force. Thankfully, Connor had deduced her involvement in WITSEC, then proposed to her a few weeks later. It had taken all of the pressure off Isabelle, who no longer had to hide things from Connor. As her husband, he was privy to all of her truths.

"Husband. I like the ring of that," Connor said as he dipped his head down and placed a tender kiss on her lips. Isabelle kissed him back with equal measure, all the while rejoicing in the blessings they'd received. She was so very thankful.

"I couldn't be happier," she gushed as the embrace ended. "God has been so good to us."

"I won't argue with you on that. He brought you all the way to Owl Creek… and to me. I'll always be thankful for it, even though I know you came to Alaska out of necessity, not choice."

"I can't imagine being anywhere but here. Right by your side. Every step along the way led me right to you." She smiled up at him, joy shimmering in her eyes. Connor was her happy ending. Her rainbow after the storm. "You and me and a lifetime of happiness."

"That's all I want, baby. For us to walk through life together. You've been through so much, and you've shown nothing but bravery and pluck."

"You were with me, Connor, and because you believed in me...in us, we're standing here right now as man and wife. You stepped out on a limb of faith, even though I gave you every reason to doubt me. You did the work to bring us together."

"You were worth fighting for, Isabelle. You're the strongest woman I've ever known. What you went through back in Miami would have destroyed most people, yet you tapped into your inner strength and persevered."

"There were times I didn't think I would make it through, but I'm so glad I did. Because of you, Connor. And what the future holds for us."

"What we have is everything I've ever wanted in this world." He took her hand and pressed a kiss on her knuckles.

Isabelle smiled as Connor's family members joined the throng of well-wishers. Her new Owl Creek family. Beulah.

Jennings. Willa and Nate. Sage. Hank. Rachel. Gabe. Piper and Braden. She was now a part of this amazing tribe of people. Although her parents, grandmother and sister couldn't be present at the ceremony due to WITSEC rules, Jonah had worked out something special to reunite them for a brief visit in another locale in a few weeks. It was way more than Isabelle had ever imagined being possible.

It was bigger than she'd dared to dream for herself. She and Connor had emerged from their struggles, stronger and more faithful. And she no longer had to look over her shoulder because she knew she was sheltered in her new Owl Creek haven. She would never be completely free from danger, but she wasn't going to be living in fear. For now and always, she would be safe in Connor's loving embrace.

* * * * *

*If you enjoyed this book,
look for these other books
set in Owl Creek:*

**Her Secret Alaskan Family
Alaskan Twin Surprise
Alaskan Christmas Redemption**

Dear Reader,

Thank you for joining me on this trip to Owl Creek. Isabelle and Connor's love story was fun to write. I hope you enjoyed it. This book challenged me in so many ways. I tried to put myself in Isabelle's shoes and found it daunting. It would take courage to rebuild your life and say goodbye to your loved ones.

Connor is a charming and caring man, whose life was shaped by the abduction of his sister. This traumatic incident left him with lingering feelings of mistrust, which complicates his relationship with Ella. I have a lot of compassion for Connor because his childhood was affected by the hole in his family, which was the result of one person's act of evil.

Ultimately, the thing that brings Isabelle and Connor together is their yearning for love. Both are suffering from loneliness and a desire to establish something meaningful with a romantic partner. Hope is a thread that runs throughout the story.

I love writing inspirational romance for the Love Inspired line. I'm blessed to do what I love. You can find me on my Author Belle Calhoune Facebook page, as well as on my website belle-calhoune.com.

Blessings,
Belle